Bows & Bitter Betrayals

Shady Creek Small Town Cozy Mystery

Renee Lyles

Contents

Introduction

Blackmail and bitter betrayal are a deadly combination.

Pastry Chef Maggie Wilkerson is anxiously awaiting the grand opening of her new Coffee Shop and Bakery, but finds herself trading her apron in for her detective hat.

Tag, who just recently escaped charges from a murder investigation, was trying to clean his act up. Instead, he's being investigated by the IRS for his previous schemes and business affairs.

Coincidently IRS investigator, Jonathan Gertler, has many of his own schemes going on. This time, he crossed the wrong person and it left him cold and six feet under.

Tag's innocence lies in the hands of Maggie because the sheriff still has it out for him from his last murder escape. Turns out, many people in town had been wronged by Gertler one way or another.

The mysteries are piling up and it's up to Maggie to uncover the secrets, sift through all the suspects and expose the killer hiding in plain sight.

Prologue

Looking back on it, Sheriff Wakefield regretted slowing down at all. It was partly habit, being on patrol and looking out for unusual or strange occurrences had become so ingrained that he naturally watched the town even on his rare time off. On the other hand, did a Sherriff actually ever have time off?

He checked his watch and pulled over.

"What's wrong?" Maggie turned to him and looked around. He pointed to her bakery, the one she only just opened. The one that was closed for the night. The one where someone was currently slumped over on one of the outdoor tables. "Oh no," she breathed under her words, "Not again."

He put the truck in park and unfastened his seat belt. "It's probably just someone asleep or waiting for a ride."

Maggie didn't sound convinced. "Once you've found one corpse at your place, it kind of sets you up for a pattern."

Despite himself, he suppressed a grin and popped his door open. "We have time before the movie starts." He checked his watch again. "Besides, there are opening previews and ads, so let me handle this and we'll—"

"That's Tag." Maggie exclaimed. In an instant her trepidation had transformed to worry. She threw her door open and piled out of the truck.

Of course it is. Wakefield sighed and climbed out. *If anyone was going to ruin a date, I would have thought it would be him.*

He shoved the irritation aside and strolled down the short walk to the café. Maggie was already by Taggart's side and was prodding him. From the smell alone, it was fairly obvious that Tag wasn't just sleeping, he was sleeping off losing a fight with a bottle of...gin? Maybe whiskey.

"Tag...Tag..." Maggie gave the man a push, trying to wake him.

"Let me try." Wakefield cleared his throat and slammed his hand on the table.

His method was a great deal more effective. Tag tried to jump out of his skin. He nearly over ended on the bench and caught himself at the last moment, his eyes searching wildly until they blearily focused on the pair in front of him.

"Oh." He mumbled the word, his eyelids narrowed in the squint that told the sheriff if Tag didn't have a hangover, he was well on his way to creating one. "Hey, Sheriff. Come to arrest me?"

"Don't tempt me," Wakefield said and shook his head. "I don't need the paperwork. C'mon now, time to go home. Sleep it off."

Taggart looked around as if he didn't understand where he was. "Alright..."

"Tag?" Maggie laid her hand on the other man's shoulder, "why don't you come in and have some coffee first." She gave a pointed look to her date and added, "I am sure we could all agree that would be safer for you and everyone else if you were a bit better able to...navigate."

Wakefield checked his watch. His movie date was evaporating before his eyes. He returned Maggie's glare with one of his own, but even then, he knew the outcome of that argument. He reminded himself that this was why he'd asked Maggie out in the first place. It was her compassion which had drawn her to him. Her absolute zeal for helping her friends, even when they were set on making fools of themselves.

Like Taggart here was trying to do, especially in the way he stood and swayed, catching himself on the edge of the table.

Maggie rushed in, the angel that she was, and draped one of her arms over his shoulders and led him to the front door. "A little help?" she asked and Wakefield bit back a growl of impatience. Right. He came to take up her burden while she unlocked the place.

Wakefield bit back a groan. Taggart had been a football hero back in high school. The former quarterback had not changed much since then except to thicken a little around the middle. He was still a pretty solid mass of muscle though and not easy to maneuver when drunk. The fact that the sheriff had found himself being a prop for a well-lubricated Taggart really had been the low point of the night. While Maggie took her time unlocking the door, Taggart dropped his head on the sheriff's chest and promptly drooled on his shirt.

The door opened, though not soon enough and he half led, half carried Taggart to the nearest chair. He dropped him down in it, rather unceremoniously and proceeded directly behind the counter to grab a rag and wiped his shirt with a wet corner.

Taggart didn't seem to notice any of it. He was looking around bleary eyed like he had no idea where he was.

Yeah. This makes for a romantic night out.

Wakefield sighed and watched as Maggie darted behind the counter to fuss at the fancy coffee machine she'd put in recently. He had no idea how you were supposed to get a simple cup of coffee out of something with so many knobs and valves, but Maggie seemed to know what she was doing. In no time at all he could smell coffee percolating, which was a far better smell than the distillery Taggart seemed to be carrying on his clothing.

Wakefield took a seat at the counter and ran his hand over his face. This really wasn't the night he had in mind. Taggart was really not the person he wanted to see, not after he got away with that last business. He should be in jail, not draped across Maggie the way he'd been when he'd come in. Not snoring at a table in her brand-new café, stinking up the place.

With the coffee started, Maggie returned to Tag and sat beside him.

"I made reservations..." Wakefield set the rag down and surveyed the growing wet spot on his shirt.

"I know, but..." she gestured to Tag. It was like she had seen an injured puppy, and she wasn't about to leave it, no matter what kind of dirty dog it was.

"You are a kind woman, Maggie," Taggart mumbled from across the room. He turned his head to Wakefield by virtue of throwing it back and forth on his neck until it was in the approximate correct direction. "It's nice to see someone who *cares* about the community, even when they *aren't* sworn to protect their people."

Taggart returned his gaze to Maggie in much the same way. Wakefield was half convinced that the man's head was about to leave his shoulders. It was rather disappointing to see he was wrong.

"I am sorry, Maggie."

It might have been a halfway decent apology had Taggart not belched the name. As though it were a signal, she rose and headed to the coffee pot. It wasn't quite ready, but she poured what there was, the strongest part of the brew and brought a cup back to the table. "I know I'm a burden, and I interrupted your night..." Tag raised an eyebrow as if hinting more about her time with the sheriff that was obvious. By morning, half the town would have her Mrs. Wakefield, and they would be lined up to tell the other half.

"I'm just...a drunken jerk, is what I am."

"True."

Maggie shot the sheriff a quelling look and set one long fingered hand on Tag's sleeve. "What's going on Tag? What's wrong?"

"Space Y." Taggart mumbled again, and it took total control for the sheriff not to roll his eyes and moan. His plans to build a spaceport in his empty field could send him to prison for fraud. The biggest reason he hadn't was that it had become a running joke in the community. So far, there were no charges filed against him, but there was always hope.

Taggart turned to him and said with a little more heat. "Vandalism. Someone was on my property and messed up the place. Where were you?"

"Patrolling the rest of this town. I can't be everywhere at once. I sent someone out to take a report. That should have been good enough. I need to track down criminals who move dead bodies and stick them in freezers."

Taggart subsided and returned to his coffee. "Wasn't too bad, I suppose. I mean...it wasn't much...just..." he faded off into a world of caffeine and remorse. Maggie shushed the sheriff. Maybe she had the right seeing it was *her* freezer the body was stuffed into. At the same time, he wanted to point out that though Tag didn't kill him, he had been an accomplice. Wakefield was still upset the man eluded jail time.

"That can't be the reason you're..." Maggie waved a hand to indicate the state Tag was in.

"No." Taggart drew out the word. "No, no, I'm being...investigated."

That got Wakefield's attention. "By whom?" If there was an ongoing investigation in his town, he should have been notified.

"EYE ARE ESS." Taggart hissed the words. "An organization more frightening than the gangs or over-zealous policemen. "They start with an audit and from there it's all medieval torture."

Maggie exchanged glances with Wakefield who shrugged. "What does the IRS want with you?"

"Space Y," was all Taggart could say. He seemed to slip away again, and Maggie caught his coffee cup halfway to the floor. The content in the cup was not as fortunate and a pool of coffee exploded at her feet, staining her skirt.

"Why don't you take him home?"

"What?" Wakefield had that momentary vision of a movie and dinner. In his mind's eye he had adjusted it to a later showing, followed by a bite at whatever was open late enough to serve them. It was dashed for the second time that night. They really were calling it a night.

Maggie set her hand on his chest and looked up at him with wide, soft eyes. He knew he was being played and worse, she knew he knew it. It was a funny sort of game to play but that made it no less effective. "I can't go like this, and I have to clean up. When you get back, we can still make dinner, after I change. Alright?"

Wakefield sighed and shook his head. "I got all dressed up for him." He looked down at his dress shirt, still kind of slobbery, and the fresh pair of jeans he'd donned just for this evening. Fine. "I'll be right back." He marched over to where Tag was snoring and pulled the man up by one arm.

Tag snorted and righted himself. "You locking me up?"

"Taking you home, Tag. You have enough problems."

"You're almost human, you know that?" Taggart patted the sheriff and turned to Maggie as though something occurred to him. "How's the dog?"

Maggie might have winced. "He's going to be just fine."

It was to her credit, she answered him when she had every right to be mad. Tag had hit that dog with his car when trying to fly under the radar after moving a body.

"I never meant to hurt a dog. I love dogs. I was panicked and...I'm sorry."

"Let's go apologize to your bed, Tag. Come on." Wakefield pulled the man through the door as Tag began berating himself for hitting the dog with his truck. It was going to be a long drive to his house, even if it was only a mile away.

"Wait, what did I do to my bed?" Tag exclaimed as Wakefield poured him into the cab of his truck.

"I have faith in you, Taggart," Wakefield assured him, "you'll do something." He closed the door and turned back to see Maggie at the door, still frowning after them like she was worried. The woman sure had a soft spot for strays. One of these days it was going to prove her undoing.

Chapter One

Mornings were not usually the enemy.

Of course, the bakery and coffee shop weren't even open yet...officially. That wouldn't happen for several weeks. Maggie considered the baking she was doing now as sort of a test run. A way to get an idea what people would want to see on the menu on a daily basis. She was also learning the quirks of the old oven and the other equipment. Making things her own.

What this meant was she could have slept in today. Given herself a day off.

Who was she kidding? She was baking because she couldn't wait for the official Grand Opening to actually happen. She liked having her friends and neighbors drifting in bright and early, eager to see what she'd produced for them today.

But I need help. I can't do this all by myself.

With this in mind, Maggie was thankful she was spending this particular morning after her borderline disastrous date interviewing possible assistants. Well, she was thankful for the foresight in setting up the appointments. She was tired, so she was starting to wonder if she was being hyper-critical or something, but no one was working out. So far, she was having trouble finding the right balance of baking expertise combined with customer service and ability to handle the counter. It seemed if she found someone who could bake well, they had no ability or patience for handling the old register. If they were experienced servers, more often than not, they proved hopeless in the kitchen. The problem was she didn't think she could manage to hire two separate people just yet, which she knew was the more practical solution.

I might just have to train someone from scratch, Maggie thought, as the most recent applicant drifted out the door. This last prospect hadn't known meringue from a mixing bowl. She yawned and rested her head on her hand, wishing she hadn't stayed up quite so late last night. She only intended to close her eyes for a minute.

"Can I get you some coffee?"

Maggie jerked awake to find a young man with dark hair and an open expression holding out her own coffee pot toward her. Stunned she could only nod, unable to find the words, watching in shock and disbelief as he filled her cup and set a fresh-baked muffin on the counter in front of her.

Maggie had not baked muffins today.

"I'm sorry, did you...?"

"I hope you don't mind if I took a little liberty in your kitchen while you were asleep. I hated to wake you, and thought, well, actions speak louder than interviews."

Interviews. Hadn't she seen the last applicant?

Maggie ignored both coffee and muffin and got up from the booth where she'd been conducting interviews and practically flew into the kitchen.

A rack of blueberry muffins stood cooling on the counter next to the stove. Strawberry rhubarb muffins rested on plates next to those. The entire kitchen smelled heavenly, of cinnamon, ginger and other mouth-watering spices.

The kitchen itself was immaculate. Every measuring spoon and wire whisk were put neatly away. Whoever this was had not only baked muffins but cleaned up his workspace. The place might have even been a hair cleaner than she'd left it.

"You made two kinds of muffins?"

"Three. The pumpkin spice is in the oven."

Of course they were. That's what smelled so heavenly. "How long was I asleep? Never mind. I was up way too late last night." Maggie grabbed a muffin from the rack, breaking it open and studying the texture before sampling a morsel.

Heaven. It was sheer heaven. "You used vanilla? Something else too...a hint of cinnamon?"

"I went with the classic recipe and maybe personalized it a little."

"What's your name?"

"Garrett Lee." The man offered his hand to shake. He seemed about her age, maybe a touch younger. His face was unlined with no hint of grey in his hair which tumbled over his forehead. Yet he carried himself with a sense of purpose, maturity which made her think he was older than he appeared.

"Can you make doughnuts?"

He blinked. "Doughnuts? What kind?"

"Surprise me." With that she spun on her heel and retreated to the dining room just as her father came in.

"Dad! Want a muffin?"

"I'd love some of that coffee more. Though I won't turn down a muffin or two." Ted Wilkerson seated himself at the counter while Maggie poured him some coffee. To her surprise the pot was quite full. How in the world had she slept through a muffin marathon, she didn't know. The fact that she'd snoozed through the coffee grinder was honestly concerning.

She really had stayed up way too late last night. "Let me grab those muffins." She started to head back into the kitchen and paused. "Wait, where's Benny? Did you leave him at home?" Most mornings, her father brought the German Short-haired Pointer to the bakery with him. The bakery is his first stop on his morning jog. She'd learned the hard way that bringing the dog in with her to work was a sure way to limit productivity, especially as she couldn't let the dog into the kitchen, and he got lonely when he was in the dining room by himself for too long.

"You'll see," her father responded with a smile.

Maggie's eyebrow arched.

"In the meantime, since you're alone, I was hoping for a favor."

"Let me get you those muffins and you can ask away."

The muffins took only a moment. Mostly she wanted to check on the new guy...what was his name? Gary? Garrett? He seemed to be engrossed in his doughnuts and though she was curious to see what he was making, she retreated with a basket of assorted muffins in hand allowing him to work rather than interrupt him.

"Okay, Dad, what do you need?"

"First...are you all right? You seem a little off."

Maggie winced. "Up late last night."

"You did get in awfully late. Not that I noticed. You have a nice time out?"

Well, that was one way to wake up. Now she was mortally embarrassed. Maggie had been living with her father since moving back home and opening the bakery. More and more she was thinking she needed to devote a little time to finding the perfect home for herself.

Soon.

In the meantime, a little damage control before her father got the wrong idea.

"We ran into Tag last night. Sitting over here kind of...well, he wasn't well..."

Her father nodded at this. "He has quite a lot on his mind right now. Not surprised if he's turning to a little liquid forgetfulness."

"Liquid forgetfulness? Dad..." Maggie only just stopped herself from rolling her eyes. "Though you're right about that. I guess he's got the IRS after him now over that whole Space Y thing. Dad, how much trouble could he be in legally if it turns out people invested in nothing at all?" She'd worried about this through the remainder of her date last night. Mindy, Tag's ex, was a friend of hers. Sort of. And they had the cutest son. "Would his family be affected if things go south for him?"

"They could be. Depends on how the articles of incorporation were written and whether or not Mindy's name was on anything. Tax law is complicated and comes with some pretty serious penalties if you're found to be doing anything wrong."

Maggie winced. "That's what I was worried about." She grabbed a muffin from the basket though she didn't have much appetite. "Let's change the subject. You mentioned a favor?"

Her father chuckled. "It's not quite a subject change, but I'll try. It's about Doxie."

"Doxie?" Doxie was the widow of the former mayor, and usually a force to be reckoned with. She hadn't seen the woman recently though and wasn't quite sure what he was getting at. "Is something wrong with Doxie?"

"I'm not sure. That's what I'm hoping you can tell me."

Maggie stared at him, trying to figure out if he was kidding or not, but the expression behind his glasses was somber, even serious. "All right, Dad, you better tell me about it."

"There's been some talk around town," he started. "People are worried about her."

"Dad, her husband was just brutally murdered. The local grapevine is going to be analyzing her every movement just to make sure she's grieving properly. I'm sure it's nothing."

Everett, Doxie's husband, had been discovered in Maggie's freezer, this was a point she didn't bring up as her father was quite familiar with the facts.

"Grieving yes. Acting...strangely though, is another matter altogether."

"She's still hunting for money?"

"You heard her. She insists Everett left her a million dollars. Hidden for safekeeping."

"If there is a million dollars, a man doesn't stuff that kind of money in his mattress unless it was obtained illegally." Maggie shook her head, then realized why her father was asking. "You've been hired by someone, haven't you?"

At that moment the door to the bakery swung open. The bells on the door jangled merrily. Maggie's gaze went to them, startled that she hadn't heard them earlier. Just how deeply had she been asleep?

A scrabble of nails on wooden floors drew her gaze back to the new arrivals. Benny, her German Short-haired Pointer, pulled on his leash, towing ten-year old Bobby Campbell to the counter. "Well," the boy asked, bending to unclip the leash so the dog could wander unhampered to his big pillow in the corner. "Is she going to help out with my grandma or not?"

Grandma? For a moment Maggie was confused before she realized that Everett had been Tag's father, hence Bobby's grandfather. Making Doxie, Bobby's grandmother. Kind of. She hadn't been married to Everett for very long prior to his death.

"She's the only one I've got left, so I've got to protect her. Hey, you've got muffins!" The boy reached across her father's plate and helped himself. "Add it to my bill," he said between mouthfuls.

"Bobby is your client?"

Her father kind of shrugged. "He wants me to look into her best interests."

There was a lot left unsaid in that statement, not the least of how Bobby was paying her father's fee. He'd been a lawyer for decades but retired. Not long ago, he'd started acting as a consultant to a select few individuals. 'Just to keep his hand in it,' as he put it.

"And I'm supposed to do what exactly?"

"Bring her some muffins?"

Maggie's eyes narrowed.

Her father smiled. "Just...be a friend."

"I barely know her."

"Then it's time you introduced yourself properly." He took a bite of the last muffin, and the conversation was clearly over.

Maggie got up to grab the coffee pot so she could refill his cup. In so doing she saw the man standing at her kitchen door. Garrett had been listening to their whole conversation. He moved back away when he realized he'd been spotted and returned a moment later with a tray of fresh baked doughnuts.

Her father and Bobby looked up in surprise as he came into the dining room and set the tray on the counter. A half dozen different doughnut types were represented on the tray. There was no way he could have made them as quickly as he had.

"I might have had some dough rising when I woke you. Just in case," he said in response to her shocked stare. "Here, let me get that for you." He took the coffee pot from her hand and started refilling cups.

Maggie grabbed a jelly-filled doughnut and took a bite.

Wow. Oh wow.

She didn't know the first thing about him.

He'd just been spying on her.

He was the best thing she'd seen all day.

"You're hired." She spoke around the mouthful of delectable good-ness. Let the chocolate chips fall where they may.

Chapter Two

I nitially Maggie thought she might wait and see if Mindy would come around to give her an excuse to see Doxie. But she had time to think that afternoon about the whole affair and realized Bobby might not have told his mother he was engaging a lawyer to see after his pseudo-grandmother.

Perhaps it was for the best Mindy didn't know.

It wasn't that Maggie was trying to hide things from her new friend. She and Mindy had been rivals in high school and their relationship still felt a bit tenuous at best. Doing anything to upset that would likely destroy whatever friendship they had formed. No, more it was to save the single mother's further heartache. Mindy's own grandmother had been arrested for murder, and the elderly woman had been a strong figure in Bobby's life up until now. The fact the boy was feeling this so keenly that he would try to supplant that person in his life with a virtual stranger spoke volumes.

Maybe it was best she left well enough alone.

She decided she would drop by to visit Doxie with a basket of muffins.

Initially this led to another challenge, one of a more personal nature. The bakery had been busy after her father left. She suspected he must have said something on social media about her new pastry chef, because it seemed everyone in town had shown up in the last couple of hours to sample Garrett's baked goods. There weren't any doughnuts left to add to the basket, and she'd been lucky to snag the last few muffins as it was.

The fact her customers raved about the new chef outweighed even Maggie's surprise to find out her father knew about TikTok and had posted a video of the muffin basket before leaving. How was she supposed to feel about this? Proud her business was taking off before even the official Grand Opening. At the same time, it shamed her a touch to find she was jealous of sharing the spotlight.

Yes, she definitely needed to get out and clear her head.

The bakery closed at 2:00 each afternoon. Since Garrett had stayed the entire morning, she gave him the task of the final cleaning and prep work for tomorrow. To her surprise, he had taken on the assignment when she still hadn't even collected his information to make him an official hire, spoke volumes about how much he wanted the job. She promised him when she got back, she'd collect his social security number and get him officially on the payroll.

He'd volunteered to enter the information himself into her accounting program on the computer if it would be more helpful.

She'd given him a look, deciding then and there one could be too eager. "I will take care of it when I get back," she reiterated and left, shaking her head.

It was such a nice day, Maggie decided to take the dog and walk since Doxie didn't live too far away. She went slowly because Benny was still recovering from the accident which had almost killed him. No. The accident where Tag had almost killed him.

She studied the dog as he walked along, pausing to sniff at mailboxes and fenceposts. He still moved with a slight limp.

Maggie's lips compressed into a hard line. For all her defending of Tag last night when she felt the sheriff had been too hard on him, she still had issues with him too. Sure, he'd apologized about hurting the dog, but she'd heard his apologies a few times now and it didn't take away from the fact that he'd acted selfishly and carelessly enough to hurt the dog in the first place. She had a right to be wary of him, second chance or not.

Still thinking deeply about this, Maggie turned the corner on the street where Doxie lived and stopped.

It was obvious from here which house was hers, even if she didn't already know.

This block was kind of upscale compared to the rest of the town. The houses here were bigger, set further back from the street, grand old places constructed of brick and stone. Even the old Victorians had been lovingly restored on this street, gleaming with care and fresh paint.

Doxie's house was much like the rest in size. Built in the early 1900s, the place held a certain style, and had been kept up well. The yard though, was another matter. It looked like a minefield, with dozens of holes dug throughout, small mounds of fresh earth next to each with no attempt to fill them back in.

Frowning, Maggie tugged on the dog's leash to keep him out of the holes and made her way to the front door.

The doorbell chimed within the house, echoing loud enough Maggie could hear it from where she stood on the porch. For the longest moment, no one came. While she was still waiting at the door, a young woman went by pushing a stroller. She paused to give a long stare at Maggie and the dog before shaking her head and moving on. It was a look which did not carry much friendliness.

Still, no one came.

"Not sure what to do here, Benny. Any ideas?"

The dog nosed the basket she was carrying. He probably wanted a muffin.

Maggie wanted a muffin.

Maggie wanted anything but this task before her because she suspected she knew what was going on and that she wasn't going to like it when that door opened. With a sigh she pressed the doorbell again.

This time someone came.

Doxie had changed since Maggie had seen her the first time. Orange corkscrew curls maybe a little duller and tangled than before. Her face seemed pale, less round. A drawn look around her eyes made her seem careworn. Her expression was dull as she pushed open the door.

"Yes?"

It wasn't the most pleasant of greeting, but could you expect a chipper attitude from someone who was grieving? Especially someone who was quite clearly looking very hard for something. Over Doxie's shoulder, Maggie noticed huge holes in the drywall at steady intervals all the way around the room.

"New puppy?"

"What?"

Maggie's smile faltered. Okay, well she wasn't in a chatty mood. She shook herself and held out the basket. "I was thinking about you today and wondered if perhaps you might enjoy some muffins. My new hire made them."

Doxie stared at the basket.

"I can just leave them here for you. For later."

Doxie tried to smile. "It's quite kind of you. Thank you. I'm..." She glanced over her shoulder. "I'm remodeling."

Maggie took a breath. So far as she could see, at this point she had two choices. The easiest would be to make some inane comment, accepting the blatant lie and go on her way.

The other was harder. It meant being a friend, even when she knew the conversation she needed to have was going to be very awkward for both of them. Maybe not as awkward as the time she had to tell her cheating louse of a fiancé that things were over between them. She'd used cherries jubilee to underscore her point.

This was still difficult though, and probably going to make the top ten of awkward conversations.

"That's not remodeling, Doxie. That's..." She waved her hand at the space behind the older woman and hoped she would be willing to at least talk about it.

The problem was, Doxie had changed. Back when the case was solved only a couple weeks ago, she'd seemed more accepting of the situation. Practical. Pragmatic even. She'd even been treating the missing million Everett had hinted at for years as a joke. Something that wasn't real.

Somehow, in the last few weeks, her attitude must have changed, for this was a woman haunted. Her pallor and intensity spoke to being upset. The fact that Doxie being only five feet tall also meant that when she'd taken a sledgehammer to the inside walls of her home, only the lower portion of the walls had been knocked out.

Not exactly what you would expect if someone was remodeling.

"Doxie, talk to me. I'm here as a friend. I want to help."

Benny whined.

Doxie's expression changed. She tried to smile. "If you don't mind coming in..."

"Not at all!"

Maggie hauled the dog into the house before Doxie could change her mind. It was worse than she'd thought. Couch cushions spewed stuffing from awkward gashes cut in the fabric. Several floorboards had been removed, making walking somewhat difficult.

This was the work of a woman desperate to find something.

Doxie motioned Maggie over to the couch, setting the basket on the coffee table in front of her before drawing up a wooden chair carefully. The feet of the chair straddled an open space where a floorboard should have been.

There was such an awful silence between them that there was nothing for Maggie to do but to take the bull by the horns. "Is it the money?" she asked finally. "The million dollars Everett told you about?"

Doxie couldn't even meet her eyes.

"Doxie, I understand. Truly I do. So would anyone else. If I thought there was a million dollars stuffed in the walls of the bakery somewhere I would probably tear them open to look too. Not—" she put up a hand when she saw the sudden, hopeful look in Doxie's eyes. "—that I think there is such a thing there. I am speaking only in theory. As far as I know, Everett would never have had the opportunity to put anything in the bakery at all. Nor any reason to. If there was any money."

Benny had been sniffing around the room while she spoke. He seemed to sense Doxie's mood though and pressed his nose against her arm until she started petting the dog almost without thinking. "I was going to ignore it," she said finally. "Then I started thinking how if the money was there, I could do so much good with it. A college fund for Bobby. Help Mindy..." Her voice trailed away.

"Help Mindy?" Maggie blinked. "Is she in trouble?"

"No," Doxie waved that off. "But Tag is. With that tax man here. I mean, Tag was Everett's son and he's in trouble. I know Everett wouldn't want him to be arrested…" She seemed to falter here. "I mean he was arrested, but again. I think it would stick this time."

Maggie secretly agreed but held her tongue.

"I just kept thinking, maybe if we paid off all of Tag's investors then no one would be out anything. The IRS wouldn't have any reason to go after him. Maybe that creepy little bald man could go back to whatever rock he crawled out from under." Doxie sniffled.

"You've seen him? He's here?" Maggie had only heard about any of this last night when Tag had told her. She hadn't been in town long enough to hear things through the grapevine the way others did.

"Did I say that?" Doxie shook her head. "I don't know why I said that." She patted the dog one last time and stood up. "Thank you for the treats, Maggie. I'm sure I'll enjoy them. But if you excuse me, I think I need to get back to work." She headed through the opening which connected the living room to the dining room. Maggie started after her until she saw Doxie had picked up a sledgehammer from where it was leaning against the wall. Doxie picked up the heavy object and with a mighty heave planted it in the wall next to the sideboard. Plaster dust filled the air, as she pulled the hammer back out, taking half the drywall with it.

Benny was hiding behind Maggie's knees.

"Right. Yeah. Um…enjoy."

With that Maggie beat a hasty retreat. On the sidewalk outside she bent over to shake plaster from her hair.

Her dad was right to be worried. So was Bobby, poor kid.

Maggie wished she had some idea what she was supposed to do about any of it.

Chapter Three

Maggie was deeply troubled by her entire encounter with Doxie. The state of the house alone seemed to be a cry for help. She would have to talk to her father about what she'd found. She supposed they would have to involve Mindy in the matter, given as how the original 'client' was certainly not in a position to be part of circumstances so troubling. And Tag! He was already so anxious over this audit. To place this burden upon him as well seemed almost unfair.

Oh, why did life have to be so complicated?

Maggie's normally sunny disposition certainly was not up to the task. She walked slowly with the dog and wondered how she could possibly help.

A pause on a street corner to wait for traffic gave her an idea. Across the way, boxes of fresh fruit flanked the entrance to Pitcairn's Market. Wallace Pitcairn himself was outside tidying up and adding several beautiful plums to the display.

Plums!

An idea formed in Maggie's head that some plum tarts would help to bring a little joy back into the world. Not that she expected something so simple as a tart to solve the problems which plagued her friends right now, but a pleasant sweet had a way of making hard things easier to bear, at least in her mind. When the light changed, Maggie made a beeline for the display, already working out in her mind just how many plums she would need, and whether or not she should add some other fruit to create a combination of flavors. Perhaps some fresh raspberries would be in order. Something more along the lines of a galette? She could do a jam from the raspberries and layer the plums over the pastry.

Caught up in her own imaginings, she was not paying anywhere near enough attention to Benny who found something much more interesting to do.

Namely, licking two very sticky children who were tagging along behind a dark-haired woman, currently attempting to fit ears of corn into a plastic bag without poking holes in the bag and thus dumping corn everywhere.

Well, at least the kids were giggling. Maggie tugged the dog away and told him firmly to sit. Thankfully Benny obeyed her without question. She gave the kids a quick look to make sure they weren't going to bother the dog before she went back to her plum selection.

"Hey! Watch your dog!"

Startled, Maggie looked up to see that things were as they had been a moment before. Her dog was sitting there, wagging his tail, somewhat confused. The children were the ones encroaching. The boy looked to be about six or seven and was holding out the remains of some bit of food to the animal, although Benny was ignoring it with the most pathetic expression she'd ever seen on the dog. The girl a couple of years younger had a saucy expression which reminded Maggie of something. Or someone. Benny wasn't anywhere near either of them. If anything, the kids looked a bit put out that they'd been pulled away from their new playmate.

"Doggo!" the girl said distinctly and flung something at Benny with a stormy glance at her mother.

The dog couldn't resist something just being offered like that and snapped up whatever it was. Maggie immediately knelt at the dog's side, worried he'd been fed something dangerous. "What was that?"

The woman flipped up her sunglasses to watch them together and sighed. "It's those blasted doughnuts we picked up at that bakery," she waved her hand down toward Maggie's pride and joy, obviously not knowing that she was talking about her bakery. "They were just giving them away."

Maggie immediately forgot the plums and everything else. "Giving them away?" She stood up, thankful the dog wasn't likely to become sick from being fed the children's leftovers. She'd told Garrett to clean up, but not what to do with any leftover stock. And besides, she thought they were out of doughnuts?

"I'm sorry, please excuse me..." she started then stopped when she realized that she knew this woman, which probably was the case with half the people in town. Only this particular individual used to be someone she'd spent a lot of time with a very long time ago. "Wait...Janet?"

It was something of a guess. She hadn't been friends with Janet since the fifth grade when they'd drifted apart, though they'd been inseparable back when they were the age of Janet's children.

The woman stared at her for the longest time before it clicked. "Maggie?"

"Yes!" Suddenly Maggie was being hugged by the smiling woman who only a moment before had been bordering on being downright antagonistic.

It was funny how time and distance could create a bond in an instant. Janet and Maggie couldn't have been further apart in high school. Janet was part of Mindy's world, all cheerleaders and football. Maggie had been into home economics and spent way too much time hanging out in the theatre, getting involved in various school productions.

In other words, their paths had barely crossed from the time they'd been thirteen until now.

But as she stepped away from Janet, she wondered if perhaps they could be friends now too, the way she was becoming friends with her high school rival, Mindy.

"What are you doing now?" Janet asked as she picked up her bag of corn and added it to her basket. "I thought you'd moved away."

Maggie hadn't been expecting this. "I didn't know you were keeping track."

"What can I say, it's a small town. I hear things. And my mom is the biggest gossiper." Janet laughed. "She keeps me up on the small-town doings. She'd mentioned you were back but hadn't been too specific about what you were doing. You took over some business downtown?"

"The bakery and coffee shop down the street." Maggie pointed in the general direction of where she'd been heading. "Probably the place where you got the free doughnuts."

"Really? Cute place. A little rough around the edges."

"We're not really open yet. The Grand Opening is in a couple weeks. I'm still in the midst of renovations. What are you up to? You make it sound like you don't live here anymore…?"

"I don't." A shadow crossed Janet's face. She glanced at the children who were sitting on the ground in a staring contest with the dog. "Visting. I think. Maybe not. Looking for a fresh start."

"I definitely know about fresh starts," Maggie laughed. "You certainly look fabulous. Like you're ready to take on the world."

She did, too. Janet was definitely overdressed for buying corn, in a designer suit and heels which Maggie suspected cost more than her rent on her last apartment.

Janet blushed, but Maggie could tell she was pleased by the compliment in the way she smiled as she touched her hair. "You like? I just got it cut...I'm not sure yet if my viewers are going to take to the short curls, but when you pair a new look with Dolce & Gabbana, you can be forgiven for just about anything." She gazed down at her navy pantsuit in apparent satisfaction. "I have to say that the hair really gives me a chance to show off the earrings though, don't you think?"

"Those are incredible earrings," Maggie said, the long loops and curls of wire in intricate design which included pearls and tiny stones caught the sun as she moved. "Viewers?"

"You know. Online? I'm an influencer."

"An influencer." Maggie had heard the term of course, but until this moment she'd never met someone who was one and wasn't entirely certain how to respond.

Janet only laughed. "I work with an organization who helps women in third-world countries build their own businesses. These earrings were made by a woman who is widowed with five children in a country on the other side of the world. I help make products like these visible, to promote the work the foundation is doing to help women like her to build better lives. Here..." Janet dug in her purse and came up with a business card which had nothing on it, but a pattern of black dots arranged in a square. "That QR code will take you to my Linktree."

The speech sounded well-practiced, but there was no denying she was passionate about what she did. Maggie didn't understand half of it. She took the card and looked at it. "You lost me back there somewhere. I really don't do social media."

Janet stared at her, absolutely horrified. "Maggie, if you intend to succeed as a small business owner, you absolutely need to have a social media presence." She took the card back, and with her left hand she wrote something on the back with a pen from her purse. "Call me. We'll do lunch while I'm here. Catch up and see if we can bring you out of the dark ages."

"I'd like that. Thanks."

She watched as Janet rounded up her offspring and disappeared into the shop to pay for her produce, then shaking her head, went on her way not even bothering with the plums.

By now, she was still worried about the bakery and what Garrett might be doing while she was gone. But she couldn't stop thinking about Doxie, she had a new concern.

Janet had seemed troubled. Maybe it wasn't in her words, but there was a sadness in her eyes as she'd turned away. And she couldn't help but notice that when her old friend had written out her phone number on the business card, there was an indented line of flesh on her ring finger. Of course, which implied something worn there typically had been recently removed.

Maggie understood that all too well. It had taken weeks of not wearing her engagement ring for that mark to go away. But then, she'd worn her engagement ring for almost five years. A relationship like that was bound to leave a mark.

She wondered how long Janet had been married and whether this 'fresh start' included a divorce.

Unfortunately, her deep thoughts also kept her from paying a whole lot of attention to where she was going. One minute Maggie was walking down the sidewalk with Benny by her side, the next she had a little bald man pressed a little too close with Benny's leash binding them securely up in unexpected intimacy.

"What in the—"

"I'm sorry. I'm so sorry...here, let me spin. No, you spin, there, go counterclockwise..." Maggie scrambled to untangle them from each other while the stranger sputtered and made some rather unpleasant comments which included digs at her intelligence, parentage, and just what kind of moron even likes dogs in the first place.

Maggie, eager to pay reparations found the man's hat, a rather businesslike fedora, in the middle of the sidewalk and handed it back to him in silence. He actually ripped the object out of her hand and slammed it down onto his bald head, glared at her from behind his glasses. Without a word, he turned and went into the nearest business, slamming the door behind him.

Maggie looked at the dog who was wagging his tail, completely unrepentant.

"You're a mess," she told the animal. "A disaster waiting to happen."

"I didn't need that to happen," Tag said as he was standing right next to her.

"I don't recall being tied up with you," Maggie responded, surprised to see him in a suit and tie, carrying a briefcase.

"No. That man was my IRS investigator. Johnny Gertler in the flesh." Tag was frowning. "Not quite the note I wanted to start this audit on."

With that, he sighed heavily and marched across the sidewalk to open the same door Gertler had gone through. The letters on the door spelled out 'Fred Morris, CPA.'

Maggie cringed. She suddenly felt like she owed Tag an apology.

And Janet could certainly use some cheer.

Not to mention Doxie. What in the world were they going to do about Doxie?

Maybe she should have gone back for those plums after all. As if a galette could fix everything.

Chapter Four

There were one or two wagging tongues that claimed Maggie's was now the new sheriff's office. The jibe was meant in good humor, though always with a bit of lurid smile. That was the way of a small town, though. The good news was that everyone looked out for everyone else. The bad news was that everyone knew what everyone else was doing.

Maggie didn't seem to be put out about it either. Certainly, Benny didn't mind if Sheriff Wakefield chose to spend his mornings, and maybe a little extra at the new bakery and coffee shop, Sweet Escapes. Wakefield leaned back in his chair, enjoying the way the dog's tongue lolled out of the corner of his mouth in the charming idiot way dogs have. The animal had taken to leaning into the ear scratches Wakefield gave him. When the sheriff stopped, Benny wagged his tail and ran to his bed to grab a tennis ball and dropped it on Wakefield's foot.

"Careful," Maggie growled, but the smile on her face gave away the humor she saw in the exchange. "I don't need tennis balls in the bread or shattered cups."

Wakefield grabbed the ball and spoke to the dog. "She's a meanie, isn't she? Huh? Spoiling your fun?" He rolled the ball the length of the room. It didn't go very far, but Benny jumped after it as though it were a runway.

Having retrieved the ball, Benny carried it back to his bed and collapsed, apparently pleased with his allotted exercise. "You didn't think he was going to give it back to you, did you?" Maggie teased. "He gave it to you once and you threw it away. He's not taking that chance again."

Wakefield chuckled and spared another glance at the dog who was busily trying to tear the wrapping off the ball with his teeth. Maggie set the coffee pot down on the counter. Her gaze turned to something other than the dog.

"I don't know who to get in touch with."

It took him a moment, but he realized she was talking about Doxie again. He sympathized with her. Doxie was one of members of the community, but his hands were officially tied. "Legally, there isn't anything to be done. It's her house, she has the right to strip the walls bare and upend the grass if she so desires."

"I'm not concerned about the house," Maggie sounded a bit put out. "I'm worried about her. If you'd seen her the way I did yesterday..."

"I understand. I really do." Wakefield reached over and grasped her hand. "And from what you're telling me, I'm worried too, but we can't actually *do* anything unless she wants help. Destroying one's own house isn't grounds for incompetence or insanity."

"It's an obsession. Everett promised her he was rich and when he died, she was expecting that money." Maggie shook her head at Wakefield's expression. "No, it's not like that...or at least I don't think it is. She really wants to help Tag."

"Tag? What has he got to do with all of this?"

"He's being audited. I met the auditor, a most unpleasant little man with an attitude. Benny over there got tangled up around us and..."

"Wait." Wakefield held up a hand. "Us?"

Maggie snorted with the memory. "I was walking him, and he got his leash wrapped around us like in that movie. Only I think I would rather be tied against a cactus than that man. I know Tag isn't your favorite person, but even you wouldn't wish that on him. Anyway, Doxie is trying to help him, Mindy, and her grandson...I really think she's wanting that money for all of the family."

"Considering that she married Everett not that long ago, that's...kind of noble, I suppose."

"See?" Maggie gave his arm a gentle back-handed slap. "Not everyone is out for themselves. There are good people still in the world." Whatever altruistic sentiment she had was tainted by the quick look he shot behind her at the kitchen.

"Alright." Wakefield sighed. "What's going on with you and the new guy?"

"Garrett." Maggie corrected him. "Nothing really, it's just...he's on probation."

"From where?"

Maggie stared at him blankly for a moment and then burst into laughter. "No, I mean, I put him on probation. I told him to close up shop when I went to Doxie's, and I found out later he's giving away free baked goods. Doughnuts and muffins. I mean, it's good advertising, but selling them is how I pay for the renovations and utilities. I can't just give away baked goods even if they are the day's leftovers. People will get the idea that if they come by at closing time, they won't need to buy the things they want."

Wakefield took a cautious sip of his coffee. "What exactly do you know about this...Garrett?"

"Absolutely nothing," Maggie admitted.

Wakefield shot her a look. "You checked his references, called his previous employer?" When Maggie didn't answer, Wakefield dropped his head into his hands. "Maggie, why did you hire someone you don't know and haven't checked out?"

In response, she dropped a small tart into Wakefield's palm. "It's called a galette. Eat it."

He studied the pastry with a dubious expression and bit a small corner. The crust was so flaky it evaporated the moment it touched his tongue. A trail of raspberries and plums filled his mouth in a burst of sweetness and spice. He took another bite and discovered that he had finished the tart and his mouth wanted more. Worse, he wanted that same experience with the first bite when the flavors seemed to caress his tastebuds and the crust melted to pave the way.

"See?" Maggie grinned at the look of rapture on the sheriff's face. "*That* is why I hired him."

Wakefield reluctantly took a sip of coffee. It seemed a shame to wash away the lingering taste of the...what was it? Galette? "I've been hearing from folks that your new man has been making friends around town since he got here."

"Well, not everyone thinks highly of him." Maggie leaned in and whispered. "I hired him yesterday and today he comes in with a black eye. Nothing too bad, but he's got a shiner over the left side."

"Did he say why?"

Maggie straightened and shrugged. "He just said that he hadn't seen a pipe sticking out of a wall and ran into it, but considering where it's black and blue, I don't see how he didn't see it."

"How about I run a background check on him for you." Wakefield paused a moment almost hating to ask the next question. "You did at least check his ID?"

Maggie nodded. "Of course. I had to for taxes. Do you need a copy? I scanned in his driver's license."

"It would help." Wakefield made a mental note. "There's a lot of folks coming into town lately. The little man in Benny's leash and your cook..."

"Janet..." Maggie nodded. She shrugged at Wakefield's blank look. "Old friend, though we kind of lost touch when we were children. I saw her yesterday at the market. She was one of the recipients of our sudden free food. Didn't look like she needed a handout either. She's an 'influencer'."

Wakefield's expression must have showed his opinion of the word because Maggie laughed. It was good to see her laugh again at any rate. "Did they all come on the same bus?" He shook his head and looked around the café. "Maybe the word about this place has reached the city and they're all coming out for the Grand Opening."

"Maybe." Maggie winked. "But we sure are busy for a place that isn't even open yet." She nodded quickly and left to go around the café and refill coffee. Wakefield watched her for a moment and took out his note pad to jot down some of the names. Especially Garrett Lee. Anyone that could make a galette like that and get into a fistfight on his first day in a new town needed investigation. If he was going to be working with Maggie, that need doubled.

He felt something on his foot and turned to see a wet, glistening tennis ball perched on the toe. Benny was sitting in front of him, his furry face hopeful.

Wakefield did have a soft spot for dogs, though Maggie was a lot more pleasant to look at. He pet Benny and played tug-of-war with the ball till she got back. "So, are we going to try and make up for the last...time out?" He tried to make it sound like a casual question, but he knew he'd failed miserably at it.

"Do you mean...date?" She exaggerated the word. He had a hard time with the word, it sounded so juvenile, so high school, but might as well call it what it is. "What's to make up for? I had a good time. The dinner was wonderful and so was the company."

"Well, then just a movie." He pushed the coffee cup toward her for a refill.

She shook her head and reached for the pot. "No. No way." She nearly laughed at his expression. "No, if I'm getting all dressed up, I need dinner with my movie."

"Deal." He took a sip. To be completely honest with himself he would likely drink dishwater just to be in there for a bit longer. "How about..."

His phone rang and he groaned. He was on duty, so ignoring it or letting it go to voicemail wasn't an option. The caller ID said it was the station, the real station where his deputies and dispatchers worked.

"Excuse me." He connected the call as he walked out of the café. He needed to take this in private and though there were only a few stragglers in the café giving them knowing looks, it was better if he wasn't overheard.

The first word that registered was Taggart and he clenched his jaw, but the rest of the call caught his attention.

"Tell him to touch NOTHING and I will be there as soon as I can. Send a car there to meet me, I've got my truck right now, but I want official vehicles there. Call the county too and let them know, we're going to need an exam."

He closed off the connection and put his phone in his pocket. There were a lot of advantages to being the sheriff of a small community, but there were some serious disadvantages as well. This was not going to be one of the good days, though it had all started so well.

He strolled back in and caught Maggie's attention. She had gone to serve one of the others who had taken advantage of his absence to put in an order.

"Can you put this in a to-go cup?" He slid the coffee to her again.

"I'll do you one better." She grabbed a paper cup from the stack on the counter and poured him a fresh one. "Is everything alright?"

He glanced around, and the nearest customer was some distance away. He leaned in over the counter and Maggie, likely warned by the expression on his face, came in close. "There's a problem at...Space Y." He felt foolish even saying that. Space Y? Not that Space X was that much better, but at least that was original.

Maggie groaned. "Oh, come on. Seriously?" She caught herself and lowered her voice. "Fine Tag shouldn't have moved the body, you're right about that. The judge allowed him to go free. He didn't kill Everett; he just did a stupid thing after Everett was killed. You have to let that go."

"It's not that..."

"More vandalism?" Maggie handed him the cup, though she was still giving him that look which spoke volumes of her disappointment in him. "He really needs a win right now. Can't you at least go out and take some fingerprints or something? Show that you're making a real effort to find whoever is doing it even if it's probably just bored teenagers or something?"

Wakefield's hand lingered over hers as he took the cup from her. "Believe me, I'd love to. But it's not so simple." He leaned in further. "Tag found a body. Murder." Maggie gasped. "At least this time," Wakefield growled, "Tag did the right thing and called it in instead of driving the corpse around town for air."

"Who?" Maggie mouthed the word. Now she was looking at the different customers in the café as if taking a headcount. Worrying about who wasn't there.

"Don't know." Wakefield shrugged. He saw the kitchen door was slightly ajar. That new cook of hers. Was he listening? He just as quickly retreated into the kitchen as he'd appeared, the door swinging shut again. Wakefield watched the door for a moment, but he did not return. Something about that he didn't like. The guy had definitely been trying to listen. "I have to go." He tipped his coffee to Maggie and headed out to his truck.

At least this time Taggart had done the right thing. He couldn't escape the feeling though that trouble seemed to follow that man the way Benny followed Maggie.

He made a mental note to check on her new chef.

That resolve was forgotten by the time he reached Taggart and Space Y. The dead man was Jonathan Gertler, the IRS investigator who'd been hassling Tag.

Chapter Five

G ertler was dead. From the moment the news broke, the bakery was packed. At this rate, no official Grand Opening celebration would be necessary – the town already seemed to know to come here for the best in local gossip.

She supposed Mindy had something to do with it. She came running in first, only moments after the sheriff had left. They'd probably passed each other on the sidewalk.

"Tag called me!" she announced, breathless. If Maggie hadn't already known, she would have guessed from the tone just how serious this all was. Mindy was near tears, her eyes filled with worry, and no small amount of despair.

Maggie remembered Mindy had loved Tag once enough to marry him. From what she'd seen, she still cared about him to some extent. Maybe you couldn't have a child with someone without having complicated feelings about them forever afterwards.

Either that or she was worried how Bobby was going to handle the fallout if Tag was arrested a second time.

"Breathe." Maggie guided her friend into the nearest chair. Behind her she heard the kitchen door open. "Get her some coffee. Sweet," she ordered, hoping Garrett would not ask questions but just do as she said.

The coffee arrived, hot and steamy, pale enough to have had milk added as well. Mindy grimaced a little at it after the first taste. "Wow. That's a lot of sugar."

"Shock requires it," Garrett said from behind Maggie, leaving her to wonder just how he'd managed to overhear her conversation with Wakefield when he'd practically whispered the news.

Mindy sat, holding the cup in her palms, leeching the heat from it to warm her hands. Slowly her face regained color. "It wasn't an accident. It can't have been. Not when it was Gertler..."

"Gertler?" Maggie asked. "Gertler the IRS guy is dead?"

Beside her she heard a sudden intake of breath from Garrett. "I...I need to get back to work." He paused, giving Mindy a long look before turning and retreating.

Maggie watched him go. "Well, that was weird."

Mindy was staring after him too. "That's your new hire?"

"Bobby told you I see."

"Yes. Garrett Lee. He looked a bit more polished when he came in for his interview. The black eye is new."

"Huh." Mindy shook her head. "Look, I need to talk to you before the whole town shows up."

"Too late."

The bell on the door jangled. A crowd came in, starting with a phalanx of little old ladies who took over the large round table in the center of the room as if they did so every day of the week. Next came a pair of young mothers, babies strapped in strollers. The room filled up and Garrett had to return just to help take orders and to plate pastries. For a bit, things were very busy, and Maggie couldn't do a thing except watch Mindy try to grow a wall around herself. She huddled more and more into her sweater until she seemed to disappear completely.

"How many people did you tell?" Maggie asked Mindy when she had a moment to catch her breath.

"No one. You. Doxie, but I was over there checking on her when Tag called. You were right about the holes. They're everywhere."

"Well, that explains it." Doxie, for all her current preoccupation, had a very large social circle.

"I'm not sure it was her. She's...so quiet right now. Not herself."

Maggie and Mindy watched the patrons, who in turn were pretending not to be watching them. Conversations stopped every time they spoke as every ear strained to hear what was going on.

"Oh, good heavens, I've had enough!" Maggie exclaimed and grabbing Mindy's hand hauled her through the kitchen door. She made a beeline for the office, shoved Mindy inside and slammed the door behind them.

Poor Benny who had been following them almost got his nose bopped in the process and sat outside whining until Maggie cracked the door enough to allow the dog entrance. She shut it firmly behind him and turned toward Mindy who was standing there blinking like she was trying to figure out what had just happened.

"Talk. You said you needed to ask me something."

Mindy sucked in a breath. "You aren't going to like it."

Maggie exhaled an exasperated breath. "Most of the time I don't even like you. Why not go for it and we'll see what happens from there?"

"Ouch. Mean girl much?"

"You would know."

Mindy stared at her then finally burst out laughing. "Oh gosh, Maggie, I needed that."

Maggie smothered a laugh of her own. "Well, now that we have that out of the way maybe we can talk?"

"Right." There wasn't much room for pacing, but Mindy walked anyway, moving in restless circles until Maggie thought she would get dizzy from watching her. When she stopped it was to draw up her shoulders, as if steeling herself for something. "What do you remember about Jonathan Gertler?"

"I should remember him?"

"We went to the same school!"

Maggie tried to wrap her mind around the idea but try as she might, she couldn't put the face of the little bald guy on anyone in her class at school. "Well, I didn't know everyone apparently. Was he in our grade?"

"A couple years behind us."

Maggie rested her hip on the edge of her desk. "That explains it then. I hate to say it, but I never paid much attention to anyone younger than us."

"He wasn't a guy who was easily liked. I remember him setting up some petition saying we should all be wearing school uniforms, exactly the same. He felt by doing so, school would quit being an endless fashion show, and people could focus properly on their studies."

Maggie could see why someone like Mindy would be horrified by such a suggestion but really didn't remember it. "So, you're saying he took things kind of seriously?"

"He took everything seriously. Had to think through every angle."

"Which would make him a very thorough investigator for the IRS." Maggie said then thought about what she'd just said, "OH! Tag..."

"Not exactly who you'd want on your audit."

"Play by the rules, dot every 'I' and cross every 't' – I can see where Tag might have a little trouble with someone like him. Things haven't been going well?"

"Not a bit. And Tag...might have been getting kind of frustrated with Gertler in the last couple days. And it might have..."

"...been Tag?" Maggie guessed, wincing. "I get it. You want my dad on standby? In case he needs help when he's questioned?"

Mindy let out a shaky sigh. "More like when he gets arrested. I mean you know how Tag acts sometimes without thinking..."

"You think he did it?" Maggie said the words louder than she'd intended and immediately forced herself to go back to speaking quietly. "I mean there's motive...and it's on his property..."

And Sheriff Wakefield would crucify Tag given half a chance. He'd had it out for him ever since the judge had opted to show leniency in Tag's case.

"Call my father," Maggie said, going to the door. "See if he can meet us at the station. I'm going to see if Garrett can take over for a bit."

Without giving away every pastry in the place.

The last part she kept to herself. Mindy didn't need to hear about her problems just then. Not when she had plenty of her own.

Chapter Six

At the station, things don't go quite as well as Maggie had hoped. For one thing, despite the growing relationship between them, Brannigan Wakefield is not pleased to see her. "Let me ask you this, Maggie. Do you trust me to do my job or not?" She'd showed up at his office door when she heard he was already back from the crime scene.

"I came to see if I can help somehow. And honestly? If it was anyone other than Tag, I wouldn't worry."

She probably sounded more than a little defensive, because Wakefield's eyes narrowed. "You seem awfully chummy with our friend Taggart recently."

"Are you kidding?" Maggie had never been more horrified in her life. Tag was...well, Tag was...a problem. Plain and simple. And honestly, right now the good sheriff sounded jealous. "I wouldn't even be here if Mindy hadn't asked me to help out Tag," she said when she found her voice again. "You know, my friend who was married to Tag at one point and has a kid with him? What affects Mindy and Bobby, affects me, because that's what friends do. They support each other."

Not that it was any of his business.

Wakefield sighed. He was pinching the bridge of his nose the way he did when he was frustrated and trying not to dig himself any deeper. Funny how in the short time they'd come to know each other, she'd already figured out his mannerisms. Nothing like two murder investigations to help you to get to know people better.

"Maggie. Please, just go home. Tell Mindy to quit bothering my staff. Don't think I don't see her over there while you're distracting me trying to get a word in alone with her dear ex-husband. That little flirtatious act isn't going to...HEY! Don't let her in back there, what are you doing?" With that he stormed past her out of the office and into the common area where Mindy was just being ushered through a locked door by one very flustered cop.

"Maggie, are you getting into trouble?"

Her dad had finally shown up.

"Not me, but I think Mindy is. Can you help them, Dad? I know you're retired..."

"But I'm kind of not. Not since you came home anyway." He chuckled when she gave him a sharp look. "We'll talk later. Why don't you make your escape before the sheriff blows a gasket and arrests the lot of us. I'll deal with all of this."

"Is Tag in a lot of trouble?"

"I don't know yet." Her father was watching an argument developing between Mindy, the sheriff, and the hapless police officer who was trying to sidle out the door. "When I asked at the desk, I was told they haven't arrested him yet, he's only being questioned. I'll make sure that none of this escalates any more than it has."

"You'd better hurry. I'm not sure that this won't come to blows." Maggie's eyes widened. Mindy was holding her purse like she was about to use it as a weapon.

Her father was already halfway across the room before she finished speaking. Maggie, feeling a little like staying was only going to put more strain on her relationship with the sheriff, such as it was, slipped out the side door of the station. She was so preoccupied she almost walked right into her old friend Janet.

Her childhood friend seemed a little less put together today. No designer suit, though she still looked nice in grey slacks and a red and black floral blouse, she seemed a touch unsteady on her heels. They were probably something horrifyingly expensive, though to Maggie's untrained eye they seemed completely impractical for wandering about town.

"Maggie! Is everything all right?" Janet immediately reached out a hand to steady her though she was the one who needed steadying.

Maggie eyed her with concern. Janet seemed a touch pale. Did her eyes seem red? "Fine. I'm so sorry. I was distracted and didn't even notice you there."

Janet laughed, waving off the apology. "Really, it's my own fault for lurking out here. I have to confess I was waiting for you. I saw you go in and wondered what was going on. You seemed upset."

This startled Maggie. "I'm here to support a friend," she said after a moment. "And to speak to one very pigheaded sheriff."

"If that's the officer who's hanging around Sweet Escapes, I'm not sure I would trust him..." her voice trailed off.

Maggie hadn't even been aware that Janet had seen him there. Hadn't she only just arrived in town? "He's been there a few times..." she answered cautiously. "Why? Do you know him?"

"I don't...think so? I mean he looks familiar, but you know how it is." Janet's laugh seemed forced. "I've been away for so long, and it's like when I saw you yesterday. It took me a minute to put your face with the girl who used to make mud pies in my back yard."

"Hey, what can I say? I always wanted to bake things."

Though it had been only a few years since they'd all graduated high school together, so it shouldn't have been hard. Maggie didn't think she'd changed all that much.

"I recognized Mindy though. I mean, when you went in. You two were together."

Maggie relaxed a little. Until this moment, she had no idea why Janet would be waiting for her. Gossip she understood. The town was fueled by it. "You saw right. If you want to wait a few, I'm sure Mindy will be out. You were cheerleaders together, weren't you?"

Janet made a face. "Don't remind me. Not about Mindy, she's okay, though I'm surprised to see the two of you hanging out. You weren't exactly friends in high school."

Well, neither were we but here you are...

Maggie squelched the thought. It was definitely uncharitable, but the longer she talked to Janet, the less she was enjoying the situation. "Situations change," she said, hoping she didn't sound too defensive.

"They do...which is kind of why I was hoping we could talk over lunch. If you're free."

Maggie almost said no, but her innate curiosity got the better of her. In truth, she really wasn't quite ready to go back to the bakery, and Mindy probably was tied up for the next hour at least. "I suppose..."

"Great!" Janet's enthusiasm was a little unexpected. It was as if her entire mood had changed with that single response. "Look, if you don't mind, I need to drop off my mom's prescription from the pharmacy and we can go right now." She held up her hand, showing off the white bag with 'Snyder's Drugstore' written on the side.

They were nowhere near Snyder's drugstore. Janet couldn't have been coming from there and just happened upon Maggie and Mindy going into the sheriff's office. She would have had to come considerably out of her way to be standing here now. Especially in those shoes.

The realization left her uneasy. "Your mom still lives over on Maple?" she asked as she fell into step beside her.

"You know mom, she'll die in that house someday. Dad built it for her when they got married."

"I didn't know that."

This launched Janet into a long story about her parents' wedding and how the house wasn't finished in time. She was a good storyteller and had Maggie laughing by the time she reached her mother's house.

It truly was a charming place, spacious but cozy with white limestone walls and a lovely front porch overflowing with geraniums. She followed Janet inside and immediately was at home. "Just make yourself comfortable. I'll be out in a minute," Janet said, leaving Maggie to explore the living room.

It was a wonderful room with a broad bay window filled with more plants. A stone fireplace took up one wall with a large mantlepiece with family photos and small trinkets from a life well lived. Built in bookcases flanked the fireplace, each side had more pictures than books. Someone here loved taking pictures it seemed.

She heard the kids laughing, and high-pitched voices babbling back the way Janet had disappeared. She expected her impromptu host would take a while. Maggie stepped around couches and chairs, moving around the room to look at the pictures while she waited.

The funny thing was, in the older pictures she saw a few which included her. Things she'd forgotten, like the time she'd gone to the lake with Janet and her family. She picked up a picture of the two of them in matching swimsuits, big grins on their faces. Maybe she was being unreasonable, feeling like Janet was wanting something from her. What if she was only looking to renew an old friendship?

She set the picture down next to one of Janet in her soccer uniform. Next to that was a picture of the teenage Janet in camo standing next to her father in similar gear. Judging from the dead deer in the picture, they'd apparently gone hunting together. Janet had been pretty outdoorsy she remembered. Hiking. Camping. Her family had been big into that stuff.

She paused at a picture showing Janet in a tank top and jeans hammering nails into a building.

"What's the context here?" she asked as Janet came back into the room stuffing something into a brown leather purse.

"What are you looking at?" She came to stand beside her and laughed. "You found my debut into the world of activism. That's from my first year in college. I got involved building tiny homes for the homeless. We created an entire community for those in need."

"Then somehow you got started into the whole jewelry thing, helping women in Africa?"

"It was a longer journey than that. It made me aware that not everyone had the benefits I did growing up." She gestured around the room at the baby-grand piano in the corner, the bits of artwork tucked between the photos. "This is all...my family is very comfortable. Not everyone lives this way."

Maggie picked up a picture of Janet holding a fishing rod with her father who held up a large fish on a line. "I love how you keep reinventing yourself. You've been so many things. I remember this girl, the one who was outdoors more than inside. Then one day, you were wearing dresses and going to proms. You went from the star of the basketball team to co-captain of the cheerleading squad almost overnight."

Janet took the picture from her and placed it back on the shelf. "There was a time I was the son my father never had," she said with a bitter twist to her lips. "Maybe my transformation did seem to come out of nowhere. But there comes a time when you finally have to decide whether you want to live a life dictated by one more man." She went over to pick up her purse from the chair. "Ready to go? I don't know about you, but I'm starved."

Chapter Seven

Maggie arrived back at the café with her mind stuffed full with new knowledge of social media she never wanted or needed. It seemed all that Janet had wanted to talk to her about was her presence on TikTok, or lack thereof. They'd ended their conversation with a promise that she would at least look at the various platforms and think about creating an online profile for the bakery and coffee shop. As if Sweet Escapes required any of that.

Well, Maggie had to concede that there was probably something to it. When she came in, at least half the people in the place were staring at their phones. Having some kind of representation on some of the more popular services probably wasn't a bad idea. It just felt like a lot of work right now when she already had a lot on her mind.

Starting with Mindy and her unlucky ex-husband.

Unless he wasn't unlucky at all, but very, very good at conning those around them.

I'm starting to sound like Wakefield, she thought as she walked through the dining room, making a beeline to the kitchen when she saw no one at the counter. "Hello?"

"Back here!" Garret shouted back as she came through the swinging door. He waved, his hands full of flour. It seemed he was rolling out cookies and Bobby was helping. Maggie stalled out entirely at the sight of the young boy in an apron far too big for him. He was applying cookie cutters to the rolled-out dough, his tongue caught between his teeth as he concentrated on pressing the various shapes into the dough.

Not that he was alone. Mindy was there too, leaning against the counter holding a cup of coffee. She apparently was talking to Garrett when Maggie came in because she started up with a somewhat guilty look, sloshing coffee over the rim and onto her jeans.

"Oh!"

"Here...let's get you a towel." Maggie grabbed the nearest cloth from the counter behind her and passed it over to her. "You okay?"

She meant the question in more than one way and tried to signify that with an odd nod to her head in Bobby's direction, which also happened to be Garrett's direction. Mindy, if anything seemed flustered by the question and shrugged. "Getting by. Garrett suggested Bobby might want to help him make cookies."

"Yes, well...I thought he was watching the counter."

"Oh, your dad has that. Tag's helping."

"Tag's...helping...."

How she had missed that, she didn't know. Maggie did an about face and peered through the doorway back into the dining room. Sure enough, her dad was standing over the table in the corner filled with a bunch of his fishing buddies. He was holding a coffee pot in one hand as if he'd been pouring refills every day of his life. Tag though was nowhere to be seen.

"I don't—"

Mindy had come up behind Tag and pointed. Sure enough, there he was. He was on the floor, apparently wiping up some sort of spill while a couple of toddlers made a game of climbing over him as their mother enjoyed her latte by the window.

"I must be more distracted than I thought if I didn't see them coming in," Maggie muttered half under her breath. "Maybe you better bring me up to date on things, Mindy. Garrett, you got those pie crusts we need for the Ladies Club luncheon tomorrow? I need a dozen total."

"Already on it." He pointed toward the counter where several pie plates were lined up neatly, a dozen crusts waiting fillings. "I'll start on filling them as soon as these are in the oven."

Well. That was...impressive. Hard to stay mad at that.

Despite this display of efficiency, Maggie was still a little put out and not sure how she felt about Garrett bringing non-employees back into the kitchen, despite the fact she did it all the time, Maggie motioned for Mindy to follow her back out to the dining room. "I want all the updates," she said, and Mindy grimaced, but followed.

Her father saw her coming and left his friends to join them after replacing the pot back on the burner to keep the coffee hot. "Glad you're back. Tag wanted to speak to both of you and I told him to wait until you came back rather than have him tell his story twice."

"Are you sure that's a good idea? Bobby will probably be done pretty soon..."

"Already covered." Her father sat down with them in a corner booth, away from the rest of the customers. "He can take Benny for a walk when he comes back. Should give us plenty of time. Tag! You done there?"

"Coming."

He joined them a moment later. Maggie noticed the lines around his mouth, the unaccustomed pallor to his skin. Tag looked tired, not that she could blame him. She imagined Wakefield probably had plenty of questions for him. She sort of hated to put him through the whole thing all over again.

At the same time, if she was expected to help somehow, didn't she need to know the details? It would be better if she heard them from Tag himself than from someone else. The problem was the patrons cluttering up the place. She'd taken the seat which would allow her to keep an eye on things, so she could get up quickly if anyone needed anything. All the same, this wasn't the most private venue.

The others seemed to understand this as well, leaning in close as Tag settled in.

"I don't know where to begin," he admitted, shifting uncomfortably in his seat.

"At the beginning...?" Maggie prompted with a look at the others who nodded in agreement.

Tag ran a rough hand over his face. "Yeah. That. You all know about the whole tax investigation I suppose. Well, it's been going rough. Three days of meetings so far. He wants to see *everything*. Wanted. Wanted to see everything. Including Space Y."

Maggie winced. Not that she liked Tag all that much, but the idea of an audit left a bad taste in her mouth. As a new business owner, this kind of thing was enough to make her cringe. Bookkeeping was not her strong suit. She wasn't quite clear on a couple of points though.

"Is there any Space Y?" At Mindy's harsh look, she put her hands up quickly to forestall complaints. "I don't mean anything bad by asking. But I'm not even sure where this property is that everyone has been talking about. Remember I haven't been here for a few years. What I'm asking is, are there buildings? Construction stuff? How far are you into this?"

Tag sighed. "Not as much as I wanted it to be. I've got...nothing."

"That's hardly fair," Mindy put in quickly. "I don't know if you remember the old hunting club out at the lake. Everett used to run the place when we were in high school, but it was really just a wild piece of land with a cabin on it. He used to stock the place with some kind of birds."

"Pheasants. Ducks. There were a couple blinds, and a deer stand. Not much else. I...um...haven't done much with the place. The cabin had an indoor shooting range setup for bad weather but mostly Dad and his cronies would sit in there talking about the glory days."

"But you took ownership of the place before Everett died?" Maggie asked, remembering that Space Y was a thing before the murder of Tag's father.

Tag grimaced. "It was always my place. Grandpa left the land to me when he died, and my dad held it in trust until I came of age. He saw no reason not to put the place to good use in the meantime."

Mindy snorted at this. "Didn't exactly want to give it up to you either when the time came."

"He came around."

"With a little help," Maggie's dad put in.

"Let me guess, you needed your lawyer hat, Mr. Wilkerson," Mindy said, her tone slightly mocking. "Seriously Tag, no offense but your dad..."

"No arguments there." Tag made a face.

One of the customers waved Maggie over. After coffee refills all around Maggie dropped back into her chair, still shaking her head. "So, back to the story? I guess this IRS guy wanted to see the building and whatever else to prove value of the property?"

Tag spun his coffee cup around in his hands. "More to make sure a business was on the property and not a residence. Especially given the zoning problems."

"Zoning?"

"The property is zoned agriculture. The hunting club wasn't a 'real' business." Mr. Wilkerson gave Tag a stern look. "We could have sorted that out if you'd come to me before launching this whole space project."

Maggie winced. "Dad, tell me you didn't just make that joke...never mind. Let's get back to what we were talking about."

"Maybe I should tell it," Mindy said, reaching across the table to put her hand on Tag's. "At least as much as I understand from what you said at the police station."

Tag nodded, slumping deeper into his chair, his expression morose. He seemed to be trying to catch his breath. Maggie looked sharply at her dad who shook his head slightly.

"Gertler wanted to see the property, so Tag went out there expecting to give a tour of the whole place. There's about 150 acres, with a long promontory sticking out into the lake. That's where Tag wanted to build the launchpad, on that strip of land. He got there about...what was it Tag?"

"About 7:00 I guess. Early."

"Right. And you said Gertler's car was there already?"

"But he was. I can tell it now Mindy. I'm okay." He paused. "I get panic attacks. Sometimes I just think I'm going to...never mind. The car. It was parked there, but looked like it had been there for a while. It was a foggy morning, remember. There was condensation on the glass and though it was parked in the grass, there were like...no tracks in. Like recent tracks. The grass was bent, but not broken. I'm not explaining this well."

"Like the car had been parked there for a while, and the grass sprang back up you mean?" Maggie closed her eyes, picturing it. "Where was Gertler?"

"I didn't know right away. He wasn't in the car so I thought he must be walking around already. I went looking up at the cabin first, but he wasn't there even though the door was open. I headed out into the fields, following the trail out to the launch pad and found him a couple hundred yards in. I mean, you could see the deer stand from there if you knew where to look."

"So, you what? Tried his pulse? Moved him somehow?"

"Never laid a hand on him. The man was dead. Arrow through the chest. I saw the blood and how stiff the body looked and grabbed for my phone. No way was I going near what I knew was going to be a crime scene. I stood back and called 9-1-1."

Tag was breathing hard as he said this. Maggie could see the uneasiness growing in his eyes, in the way he ran his hands over his thighs and shifted again in his seat. She didn't know what to do.

Mindy did. "Tag, breathe. You did the right thing. The sheriff even had to admit you hadn't done anything wrong that he could see." She glanced around the table. "He let him go. He wouldn't be here if he thought he had probable cause. Gertler had been dead for hours and he said Tag had an alibi."

Tag was already nodding. "I was playing poker with a bunch of friends."

Mindy gave him a sharp look. "Poker?"

"Just for fun."

"For money when you owe me child support?"

"You're not the only one I owe money to. I needed a big score. Thought if I won, I could..." He trailed away, his face going red.

Everyone was staring at him now.

"Tag. What else do you need money for?" Mindy asked, her voice going cold as ice. "What have you done?"

"I didn't do nothing!" Tag bolted to his feet, knocking against the table in his haste. Coffee cups rattled against silverware and Maggie had to grab her cup fast to keep it from going over.

Her father was on his feet a beat behind Tag, reaching a hand out to steady him. "Tag, stop a moment. We're here to help you. If you've got some other debts, we'll deal with it. I can make some calls, put you on some payment plans. You don't need to be worrying about that now."

"It's not like that." Tag shook him off, pacing in short circles, one hand buried in his hair until it stood up almost straight from his forehead. "It was that blasted Gertler!" Tag spoke through gritted teeth, loud enough to stop every other conversation in the room. "He told me if I gave him enough money, I could make all this go away. All of it. I was playing poker to pay him off!"

CRASH!

Every head in the place turned. Garrett was standing in the kitchen door with Bobby who must have been carrying a plate full of cookies. The boy stared at his father's white face, the wreckage of his efforts at his feet.

Chapter Eight

Wakefield took in a deep breath. The motel room he stood in wasn't particularly fresh, though it was somewhat clean. It had a certain age to it and was in desperate need of new carpet and drapes. Still, Gertler, while not a fastidious man, kept his room relatively organized. Even the manager of the motel, John Harding, couldn't complain about the mess, and John was one who lent himself to complaining rather easily.

Still, the room was stuffy, and getting outside helped to clear his head. The few cars that went by sailed past the old motel as though it wasn't there. Small towns did not have a great need for hotel space. He was fairly sure if he asked around here, most, probably had forgotten the place even existed because of the way it was tucked back from the highway. But there was enough customers to keep The Wayside in business even if half the rentals were by the week.

Thankfully the place wasn't busy right now. The last thing he needed was to contend with residents trying to get the latest scoop on the investigation. With any luck, the locals were intimidated by the way his squad car commanded three spaces. He told himself it was part of securing the area for examination. Mostly it was to keep outsiders at bay.

The bustle of forensics and the high-paced frenzy of investigators photographing and cataloging everything was over. The techs had gone back to their labs to sift through the findings. Now they had to wait until a judge gave them permission to confiscate the dead man's possessions.

Secretly, Wakefield liked the solitude of the moment. He felt as though he might be able to start looking for things logically. It was so much easier to concentrate without a crowd.

A movement from the street caught his eye and he recognized Maggie's car turning in the driveway. As it left the street and pulled in next to his, he felt a moment of annoyance. After all, it was the first time he'd been alone in the room, and he needed to do his job. On the other hand, it was Maggie and seeing her always made him feel good. He decided that anyone else would have been an interruption, but Maggie...well she had some good thoughts sometimes too. When she wasn't interfering with his investigations.

Still, it wasn't hard to smile as he walked up to her car. "Hi, Maggie."

"Hey." She bit her lower lip for a moment and continued in a rush. "Listen," she said as she turned off the car. "About what I said earlier..."

"No." He stopped her there with an upraised palm. "I apologize. I'm really sorry about.."

"Me too." She smiled up at him and suddenly they were back on their date and whatever rift they had was healed. It was like that with Maggie. She just seemed to make things better whenever she was around. It was a certain kind of magic she had. "So, what's with all the tape?" She pointed to the yellow police tape that fluttered over the door to room 12.

"Gertler's room." Wakefield leaned against the car and took a survey from the parking lot. "Just looking for evidence. It's been a full day already, had half the county in there taking pictures and lifting prints. It'll be a bit before they process everything. I was just taking a last look around before leaving."

"Could you use a fresh pair of eyes?"

She seemed awfully eager. Wakefield suppressed a chuckle. People who didn't have to do this often considered it fascinating, and maybe it was. After a while, procedures like this were just part of the job. At this point, he would rather be on patrol somewhere.

"I would like that, but you might interfere with the scene."

"You said they already did the prints and pictures. If I don't touch anything, no one will know I was there. Even if I did, *which I won't,* the evidence is already assembled, isn't it?" She lay a hand on his. "Please? I would love to see it."

He shook his head. Maggie was a smart woman, and it did sound reasonable. It might be against procedures, on the other hand, she was right about getting a fresh perspective. "Alright, fine, but you're taking precautions if you're going in there."

When Maggie smiled like that, she looked like a kid getting ice cream. She opened the car door and nearly bowled him over getting out. "Like what? A hazmat suit? Oxygen tank?" Whether she was teasing him or not, he wasn't altogether sure.

Wakefield lifted one foot and showed the bright blue disposable booty he had on over his shoes. He walked over to the door of the motel and picked up a box from the ground and offered it to her. She looked somehow disappointed and as she pulled one free and examined it. "Not quite as glamorous as what we see on TV, huh?" she asked and he chuckled.

She made a face and retrieved a second booty from the box of questionable footwear. He didn't even mind when she grabbed his shoulder for balance as she slipped them on over her tennis shoes. It was a good thing she wasn't inclined to wear heels, as they would have ripped through the bottom of the elastic cover.

She stood upright and struck a pose like she was modeling the latest fashion and he silently held up one finger. He reached down for the next box and offered her two of the Nitrile Gloves. She giggled as she slipped one on and snapped the other. Her eyebrow shot up in a challenge.

"Alright." Wakefield grinned. "Alright, but remember, *do not touch anything*."

She held up a hand with her pinky finger held down by her thumb in the classic boy scout salute. "I promise." He had his doubts about her membership in the scouts, but he took it as an oath and ducked under the tape and back into the room. He held the tape up for her to slip through.

"Why is there dark dust everywhere?" Maggie was looking around at the television and the dresser. She reached out briefly, but before he could caution her, she withdrew her hand. It looked as though she was going to give the room the white glove treatment. He gave her credit for stopping herself in time.

"That's the dust they use to lift the fingerprints."

"They use dust?" Maggie sounded surprised. "I thought...I don't know, spectral analysis or radon carbon dating or something out of a cop show..."

"Maggie." Wakefield stopped her. "Out here?" He lifted his arms to indicate the small town. "We're lucky we have radios in the squad cars. At that, I had to call in a team from another town. We just don't have that much of a need for it."

"Well, that's a good thing, anyway." Maggie was peering under the bed. "Looks like someone has a collection of dust bunnies."

"They're hiding from the maid service," Wakefield agreed. He was looking at the mirror that hung on the wall beside the bed. It was old enough to have a silvered back, though he doubted it was actual silver. The glass and the backing had begun to separate.

"Did the maid make the bed?"

Wakefield turned and regarded the furniture in question. "No. when we got here, the bed was made, and no one had been in here all day."

"Considering the state of the carpet, I would guess it's been at least two days." Maggie tutted. "I mean...unless Harding is running a flop house, which I find hard to believe, the maid service should be in every day."

"It is. I checked with him earlier. Why?"

"Well," Maggie pointed to the carpet, "this hasn't had a good vacuuming in a while. Was the 'Do Not Disturb' hanging on the door when you arrived?"

"As a matter of fact, it was." He was getting interested now. Maggie was right about a fresh pair of eyes. "What are you getting at?"

"A man who refuses maid service but makes his own bed?" Maggie bent over the mattress. "These pillowcases look fresh."

Now that she brought it to his attention, there were no creases or dents in the pillows as there would be if someone had slept on them.

"So, he fluffed the pillows?"

"Maybe." Maggie shrugged. "I don't know why, but they just look like they're fresh."

Wakefield hummed. "We'll look into that. Thanks."

Maggie grinned. "You're welcome." She took another look around. In the bathroom, she bent over the trash can. "He really needed maid service too." She nodded at the small pile in the can. "He ran out of shampoo and conditioner. That's a fairly good brand too, Harding has good taste. The soap is nearly gone too. He had to be hiding something, something he didn't want the maid service to find."

Wakefield shrugged. "Some people get paranoid about their things being gone through by strangers."

"True. I'm finding it...harder than I thought it would be to allow someone else in my kitchen."

"Garrett?" Wakefield recalled he was supposed to run a background check on her newest hire, but hadn't had the time yet. But the man was as good a cook as he'd claimed, and Maggie's place was already becoming a community gathering place and she wasn't even officially open yet.

"If you're still questioning the hire, I might point out you needed the help."

Maggie sighed. "I know. It's not a bad position to be in, so successful to have to hire someone already. It's still an adjustment, though."

Maggie made a visual sweep over the room. She pointed to the desk and the laptop sitting open on it. "So, what did you get out of that?"

"Haven't checked it out yet," Wakefield admitted.

"It seems to me like you'd go there first. I mean people keep their lives on their computers. And what is PAC10Drive$?" She pointed to a strip of masking tape adhered to the keyboard. The strip and keys were all covered in the same dust. It was the first place fingerprints were taken from.

"We're assuming it's his password."

"Really? What good is a secret password if you're going to set it in a prominent location? That's strange."

"Some folks can't remember things like that. Heaven knows I struggle to remember them all."

"Not that." Maggie looked around again. "That someone who would leave his password out and run out of basic hygiene, would bother to make his own bed..." She sat at the desk. "Shall we see what's in there?"

"Don't touch it!" Wakefield called out. He took an involuntary step toward her. "There are procedures to be followed. I need to have a search warrant for that. Harding is the owner of the motel, he let us in to the room now that Gertler is dead, but that laptop needs its own warrant to search. It's on the way. When I have it, I can turn it over to the tech team and let them sort out what's on there."

She made a face, that was a half pout, all disappointment. "Well, at least tell me what you find. I'm dying of curiosity."

"I promise..."

"Sherriff?"

Harding was at the door as if he had been summoned. "I have the list of names you wanted." He held a piece of paper in his hand. "These are all the folks in nearby rooms last night." Wakefield headed to the door and took the paper from the man through the police tape.

"Thanks, John." He paused noting the way Harding wasn't seeming in a hurry to go back to his office. If anything, he seemed ill at ease, shifting from one foot to the other. "Was there something else?"

"Sherriff, I mean it's a tragedy and all, and I'm really sorry the man is gone. But I need to get this room cleared. How long till I can get someone in here and reopen? There're only twelve rooms in the place. Losing one is a significant loss of income." Harding was trying to see past him and into the room.

"It shouldn't be long now, John." Wakefield tried to sympathize with the man. Gertler's credit card was on file at the office, and he had no doubt that Harding was going to charge the card for the lost days and take a cleaning deposit for the mess forensics had left behind. He was hard-pressed to give the man his condolences for the room being unavailable.

Harding was looking past him, likely at Maggie. Wakefield shrugged. "She's a special consultant, helping on this case."

Harding nodded sagely. "I get it. Huh. I didn't know she was a computer expert."

"Comput..." Wakefield turned as the laptop gave a happy little chime and the screen flared to life. He took a step as a spreadsheet formed on the monitor and he slammed the lid down. Maggie jumped back.

"Don't. Touch."

"I though she was a consultant," Harding said from the door.

"John. Go away or I'll have the whole place declared a crime scene for the next month. Every room."

Harding vanished like a ghost.

In the meantime, Maggie was eyeing the laptop the way a cat would a mousehole.

"DON'T. TOUCH!" Wakefield pressed the lid down tighter and wondered just how you would tell a woman to get lost that you hoped to take out to dinner later.

Chapter Nine

It was pretty clear that Sheriff Wakefield was none too pleased with Maggie. She'd jumped a mile when that lid came snapping down on the laptop. Of course, she'd kind of overstepped a bit by looking. In her defense, she didn't know how anyone could not have looked in that moment. The laptop had been right there. And he'd even said he had a warrant on the way. What difference did it really make if one looked now or later when you knew you were going to have permission at some point anyway?

Okay, maybe that reasoning was a touch shaky.

"I was just—"

"I know what you were just, Maggie. But as much as I'm fond of you, I can't have you spoiling my investigation."

Fond of her. He was fond of her. The phrase sang in her head. They'd only gone out on a handful of dates, and not all of those had ended well. The fact he still liked her felt good at a time when she hadn't had a lot of wins lately. Maggie gave him a sunny smile. "I understand completely. Though when you do get that warrant, I'd pay special attention to that spreadsheet that was open. I mean, the man did work for the IRS. No one likes being audited..."

"Especially our own Taggart?"

"Brannigan..."

She hadn't used his first name much, not entirely being accustomed to it. It startled Maggie now when the word slipped out. It likewise caught the sheriff off guard enough that his professional mien slipped and for a moment he looked at her differently, his eyes a little softer. The lines around his mouth eased. "I know you're trying to help Maggie. Why don't you go home and let me do my job. Please. Tomorrow we can talk."

"Lunch maybe?" she asked and was pleased when he nodded.

They would be okay.

In the meantime, she had things to do, starting with writing down the names she'd seen on that spreadsheet before she forgot them. She slipped out of the room, no doubt giving the poor sheriff a measure of relief to see her go. He held up the crime scene tape for her to slip under, but she could see his mind was already miles away. He kept looking into the hotel room, staring around the dingy space like he was missing something and couldn't quite lay a finger on just what it was.

Which made two of them. She'd been feeling that way all day.

***

That night Maggie was sitting at her laptop when her dad came in from spending a night out with his friends.

"I'm surprised to find you still up."

"Busted, Dad. Were you seriously playing poker all this time?"

Her father laughed as he shrugged out of his coat. "Well, we might have gotten caught up in reliving the good old days a bit."

"Good old days!" Maggie scoffed. "You're not that old dad. Barely past 65."

"Listening to Marv and Johnson talk about good old days then. They were both on city council back in the 60s and 70s. Interesting stories they've got to tell. This town has seen a lot of change."

Maggie looked up sharply. "They probably know more about that old hunting club then, where the murder took place."

Ted moved about the kitchen, filling the coffeemaker with water and adding grounds. "Probably. Would have belonged to Everett's father back then. I'm not sure you remember him."

"I don't. I didn't exactly run in the same circle as Tag back in high school. I doubt if I ever had a chance to meet much of his family."

She glanced back at her laptop and sighed. "Dad, how are you at tracking people down?"

"Who are you trying to find?" He pushed the button to start a pot brewing and took a seat next to Maggie at the table.

She slid her laptop over to him. "I was able to...well, never mind what I was able to do today..."

"Why do I sense you might need legal counsel again soon?"

"That depends on Brannigan...Wakefield." Maggie flushed. "He was mad, but I think he's letting it go."

"Maggie..."

Maggie was very familiar with that long-suffering tone. "I know, I know. I just...I'm trying to help Tag out."

"And you don't think Sheriff Wakefield is?"

Maggie stared at the notes she'd been scribbling. Scraps of paper littered the table. "I'm not sure." Much as she hated to admit it, Janet's cryptic statements had left a lingering trace of doubt in her mind. How well did she know the sheriff? How well did anyone? Mindy had been teasing her about dating the most elusive eligible bachelor in town. Was he so focused on his career he hadn't socialized much until she came along? Or was there something else which left him silent and taciturn?

But not with me. He loosens up when we're together. We talk.

Maggie got up to pour them each a cup of coffee. Her dad had made the real stuff, not decaf. Given the late hour she looked askance at him as she went to grab the half and half from the fridge.

"It looks like you have a long night planned. I thought I could help," he said, adjusting the screen of her laptop in front of him. "What am I looking at here?"

"You sure? It's pretty late."

"Getting older doesn't necessarily mean getting better sleep. Half the night I lay awake and stare at the ceiling anyway. Besides, maybe if I help you out, you can get to bed at a decent hour."

She glanced at the clock over the kitchen sink and grimaced. "I think that ship sailed a while ago." She brought the mugs to the table and sat down. "I looked at Gertler's computer and saw a spreadsheet with several names on it. Unfortunately, I only had a few seconds to look, and can't remember more than three names. These here." She slid a piece of paper over to him.

"I don't think I want to comment on how you came to be looking at Gertler's computer, but you know you're in trouble if Wakefield decides to make an issue of it."

"I know dad. But it's...well, it's important."

"So is staying out of jail. Just...be more careful, okay?" He picked up the piece of paper and scrutinized her handwriting. "Help me out here. I can't read this scribble. I see a Sid Monroe? Malone?"

"Montrose. Sid Montrose. Hurley Watkins. Holly Clinton."

"Hurley? That should be easy. Not too many people with that name. The others...well, let's see what we can find." He tapped a few keys on her keyboard. "I think we can start with ruling out anyone from out of state. While it's always a possibility that Gertler's previous clients might have moved out of state, we'll assume what's logical. Most people don't venture too far from where they start, especially if they're in financial difficulty."

Maggie leaned in to look at what her father was doing on the computer. "How do you figure that?"

"That they don't go far? Cross-country moves are expensive."

"Financial difficulty."

"It follows. We're looking for someone who isn't happy with Gertler who likely came into contact with him in his official capacity. Meaning they were being audited for some reason or another. If an audit goes badly, generally it's because you've been hiding your financial situation or trying to do something maybe a touch dishonest in your bookkeeping. Either way, you can probably assume they're having cash flow problems." He laughed at her expression. "Yes, I said 'assume.' But the best investigations start with ruling out the obvious. Saves a lot of work later on."

She stared at him, as if seeing her father for the first time. "The way your mind works is terrifying."

"But handy if you're a lawyer." He hit a few more keys. "And if I'm not mistaken, I've found your first victim." Ted slid the laptop back over to his daughter.

"Victim?" Maggie studied the article on the screen. "This is an obituary."

"Recent." Her father pointed at the date on the bottom of the page. "Two months ago."

"Doesn't that rule him out?" Maggie asked, scanning the information on the page.

"Not necessarily. It looks like he left behind family." He tapped the screen where the list of survivors began.

"People who might be upset at the loss of their loved one. That's if they have a reason to be upset…" Maggie was starting to get the hang of this. She opened a fresh tab, typed in Sid's name, the month of his death, and the location where he lived. A moment later a news article appeared on the screen. "Suicide."

Her father gave a low whistle. "A reason why someone might be upset about his death."

Maggie stared at the screen. "Would someone kill themselves over a problem with the IRS?"

"If the IRS investigator is extorting them, they might."

The very thought gave Maggie chills. "Dad, I don't like this."

His eyes were serious behind his glasses. "We don't have to do this. We can put it all into Wakefield's hands and walk away."

But Mindy had asked her. And Bobby needed his dad. Tag was innocent, but he was rattled, and definitely not looking good lately. With Gertler dead and the cops looking at him, well a man like Tag could become desperate.

Suddenly Maggie very much wanted to know why this Sid person had committed suicide. And whether Gertler had anything to do with it. "We could talk to Sid's family. The obituary listed a wife and a brother."

"Already checking." Her father had the laptop and was hunting using the search engine again. "No luck on Sadie Montrose, but I've got him. Gil Montrose. Even found a phone number."

Maggie glanced at the clock. It was going on three. "We'll have to call in the morning."

"Which is my cue to try and get some sleep." Her father got up from the table and kissed her forehead. "Let me know if you want me to hunt down those other two people with you in the morning."

She stared at her empty coffee cup. "I'll let you know. I think I'm going to be up a bit, at least until the caffeine wears off. Maybe I'll see if I can find the other two. With the tips you gave me I shouldn't have too much trouble hunting them down. As you said before, a name like Hurley should be easy enough."

"That's my girl." He squeezed her shoulder in passing. "Night, pumpkin."

"Night, Dad."

Maggie yawned and stood up to stretch after her father had gone. Idly she drifted over to the sink to rinse out her coffee cup, thinking about poor Sid Montrose. Whoever he was, whatever he'd been suffering, it was sad that he'd felt so trapped by it that he'd taken his own life. It made her wonder just what kind of man Gertler had been.

Under the kitchen table Benny was snoring. The dog's paws were twitching as he slept, likely dreaming of a day at the park or something equally innocent. Dogs had it easy. She smiled, glad that Benny had come into her life.

As if in an answer to her thoughts, the dog lifted his head suddenly, ears twitching, expression alert.

He was staring at the kitchen door which led out into the backyard. "Whuf."

The soft bark broke the silence of the kitchen. Something was out there. Or at least the dog thought something was out there.

Three o'clock in the morning. The entire neighborhood was dark and still. A glance out the kitchen window showed nothing stirring. Or at least nothing she could see when the shadows were so dark and the light from the kitchen behind her made it near impossible to see anything.

A jingle of tags behind her told her that Benny had gotten up from the old blanket he liked to sleep on when he was in the kitchen. He padded over to the back door and stood there, head tilted slightly as if he was trying to figure something out.

Maggie reached a hand out and flicked the light switch by the sink, plunging the room into darkness. Or some semblance of it. The kitchen table was lit softly in the glow of the open laptop.

Benny. Where is Benny?

In the yard nothing moved.

"What is it, boy?" she asked softly but the dog only circled back around her and with a sigh went back to his blanket and lay down.

Cautiously Maggie went to the door and put her hand on the knob. *Someone died for being in the wrong place at the wrong time.*

She withdrew her hand and instead reached for her phone which was sitting on the kitchen table. Would it be overkill to call 9-1-1? She thought about calling to her father, but if someone was out there, she didn't want to alert them to the fact that she knew they were there.

Under the table, Benny was still staring at the door but seemed less concerned. Less concerned was not the same thing as not concerned at all.

Maggie dialed the phone.

Chapter Ten

I t was a good thing she'd hired Garrett.

Maggie slumped at a booth in the dining room with her laptop. Her elbow rested on the table, in her hand was an untouched cup of coffee. Drinking it would probably have been the better choice if she wanted to wake up.

Right now, she needed all the help she could get. The police had taken ages to show up last night. Thankfully, she'd convinced them not to call in Sheriff Wakefield when a quick search of the property had found nothing at all. By the time they'd left, Maggie was fairly well convinced she'd imagined the entire thing. It had also been way past her bedtime.

Now with the morning baking needing to be set out for her first customers, Maggie was having trouble staying awake. Garrett had been the one to send her into the dining room with a fresh croissant and cup of coffee, saying it was better for him to finish up, especially when she'd tried to mix up the salt with the sugar for a second time.

I really am thankful to have the help, she thought as she twisted her coffee cup in her hands. *If only I was sure I could trust him.*

Maggie sighed and looked at the clock. Still too early to call the brother of Sid Montrose. What was his name? Gil?

To kill time, she went back to tracking down Hurley Watkins.

So far, she'd found nothing. Which was to be expected since for the last ten minutes she'd been searching for a *Harley* Watkins, not Hurley thanks to autocorrect. As it turned out, there wasn't a whole lot to find. A short article mentioned he'd been charged with fraud and where he'd been imprisoned. That particular tidbit felt like a dead end. How was she supposed to talk to a man in jail? Could you even do that?

She spent another fifteen minutes on the website for the prison trying to figure out visitor regulations and got even more muddled. Some prisoners you needed special permission to see. There were lists and things, unless you were law enforcement you just weren't getting in. But nothing told her which inmates needed that kind of permission and she felt more confused than ever by the time she went to unlock the front door and admit the first customers of the day.

If I'd had slept, this wouldn't be anywhere near so hard.

"Maggie! Hi!"

A trio of women in matching spandex and legwarmers bounced into Sweet Escapes, full of chatter about their morning. Maggie found a smile and pasted it on, bustling about to fill their orders. Once coffee was safely served to the jazzercise crowd, she was relieved to see them head out the door to their class. Much as she enjoyed seeing the ladies, their high energy was too much for her today. Her head was buzzing, and she was seriously thinking about going home for a nap.

Instead, she sat down to stare at the laptop. Holly Clifford. She was looking for Holly Clifford, right? No. Not Clifford. Clifton? Now she couldn't remember.

She had just typed the name into the search bar and found a match with a social media profile. But it wouldn't let her look without an account. She was trying to set up a profile when the bell over the door jangled again. This time it was Janet. She waved as she came over, pausing to give the laptop a very significant look. "Well Maggie Wilkerson, do my eyes deceive me or are you on social media?"

"Not in the least. I was just..." She paused, unsure why she didn't want to talk about what she was doing. "Looking up an...old friend. I really don't know what I'm doing. I guess I need an account to see her profile?"

Janet plopped down opposite her, already shaking her head as if she'd been confronted with the greatest tragedy known to man. "Now Maggie, it's really not all that hard."

"Yes? Then why am I stuck on the login page?"

"Here, give me that! You realize I do this for a living, right?" Janet took over the computer. Her fingers moved so rapidly over the keys Maggie wondered how she didn't have to keep going back to correct mistakes the way she did. She shook her head and went to fetch coffee for them both.

"Business page or personal?"

"Does it matter?" Maggie asked. "I mean if I want to look up a friend?"

Janet stopped typing to stare at her. "Does. It. Matter? I arrived just in time. Personal profile for friends. But you need a business page for Sweet Escapes. How can you possibly expect to succeed here if no one knows you exist?"

Maggie gestured around the café. "You're here. Half the town is here. The Grand Opening isn't for a week."

"Not the point!" Janet muttered, going back to her typing.

"It kinda is the point," Maggie said and shook her head. "Knock yourself out. I'm getting us some cinnamon rolls."

"Ooooh....Yes please!"

Garrett was just frosting the rolls. Maggie paused to help and by the time she came back out, Janet had fourteen tabs open and seemed inordinately pleased with herself.

"I've got you an Insta and Facebook. I added in LinkedIn because you never know, and a few other sites." She reeled off several names, showing her the corresponding tabs. "You'll notice I posted a couple pictures on everything, just a few pics I snapped from around the dining room, but you really ought to give some behind the scenes videos or something. Maybe film that helper of yours baking something? Men who are chefs are *trés chic*. I also already friended you and will throw up a post about this place on my socials. I have 150,000 followers so with a little encouragement we'll get some people reposting and see if we can get you up to speed in a day or two."

Maggie stared at the computer screen. "Wow. I mean...wow. Thank you? But what in the world am I supposed to do? And how do you make those little, short videos? And posts? It seems like it's a lot of work..."

Janet smirked. "It is. You learn the tricks fast enough, and if things take off, you can always hire someone to do your socials. Get a high school student to post daily. I can bet there's a couple dozen people going to high school who would jump at the chance. It really doesn't have to be hard."

"But you do it all yourself?"

Janet laughed, though there was something in the sound which didn't ring true. "Well, I've had to have help from time to time. It's hard when you're trying to get your profit margin high enough you can leave your lowdown husband. Especially when you've got kids to support. Most banks don't think highly of 'influencer' as a career definition when trying to buy a house."

"But isn't it also kind of dangerous? I mean putting your name and face out there like that?"

Janet laughed. "Are you kidding? I wouldn't dream of using my real name. I'll do some likes and comments later when I make my post about the bakery, and you'll see what I mean. I had to come up with something a little more elegant than just 'Janet.' The people who buy the jewelry my organization sells are generally pretty affluent. They expect me to...well, appearances matter."

"Smoke and mirrors? Show them what they expect to see?" Maggie asked and Janet flinched.

"Nothing fake about it. You need to be authentic when you're online."

"Under your assumed name..."

"Well, the rest of it is real enough. My followers have seen my house and how I live. I set very high standards and as a result I attract the sort of viewers who maintain those same standards."

Maggie shook her head. "Too complicated for me. But thanks for setting things up." She looked through the tabs again and was horrified to find that the pages about visiting the prison and the search of Hurley's name was still up. Maggie closed all open tabs and slammed the lid of the laptop down. "I'm going to go through all that later. More coffee?"

Janet gave her an odd look, as though trying to read something in her face. "No, thanks. I was just passing through. I have to get back home. My mom...the kids..."

With that, Janet wasted no time in gathering her stuff and leaving. She waved from the door but was so distracted, Maggie wasn't sure she even noticed her answering farewell.

Maggie bit her lip. Great, Janet had seen everything. At the very least she knew Maggie was planning on visiting the prison.

Maggie thunked her head down, nestling it in crossed arms on the tabletop.

It would probably be all over town by noon. Just wait 'til Wakefield heard all about it.

I'm dead.

Chapter Eleven

T he town square wasn't all that far, and the day was sunny and warm. For Sheriff Wakefield, it meant leaving his truck at Maggie's, but he had already let dispatch know that he wasn't available for a while. He needed to stretch his legs and being with Maggie was always a pleasure.

"It's a little lunch place," he was explaining to her, "I used to eat here every day, until a certain bakery opened. Now I tend to hang around there on my lunch."

Maggie raised an eyebrow and the corner of her mouth lifted like it did when she was about to say something cheeky. "You know I could have fed you today too."

"Yeah, but this time you don't have to cook, there will be no dishes to wash and, most of all, you get out of your bakery and into open air. This one is on me."

He gestured toward their goal and Maggie burst into laughter. "Are you sure you can afford such a place? I wish I had known, I feel underdressed."

"Don't be catty." Wakefield couldn't help but smile. She was comfortable enough with him to tease him a little. "I will have you know that Roberto has the finest food truck in three states. So, the napkins are recycled cardboard, but the food is fantastic."

"Cubano?" Maggie came skidding to a halt when she saw the menu board. "They have Cubanos?"

"And the BBQ beef will melt before it hits your teeth."

She stared at the menu, she must have read it three or four times. She began bouncing a little on the balls of her feet and he could see the child she must have been once. "I tell you what," he said to break her indecision. "Get a BBQ and a Cubano and we'll split them. That way you can try a little of each."

"It smells wonderful," Maggie admitted.

That it did. Wakefield's stomach growled as he ordered. He hoped she didn't hear and covered by indicating a nearby bench.

"Linen tablecloths." Maggie gingerly picked up a discarded napkin and brought it to a nearby trash can.

"All right. I warned you it's not fancy, but" Wakefield held up a hand, "wait till you taste the food."

Maggie stood next to the bench and looked between it and the trash can. "That's what...four feet? At most? They couldn't take it four feet?"

Wakefield was spared the rest of her justifiable righteous indignation when Roberto called out that their food was ready. He quickly jumped up to retrieve the paper wrapped sandwiches, juggling them from hand to hand because they were so hot. One Cubano perfectly toasted and packing more cheese than a pizza. One BBQ beef that smelled and tasted as though it had been marinating for decades. They came with a small side of fries that were chip crunchy on the outside and warm and soft on the inside. And as always, there was just the right amount of salt.

He watched as she picked up that sandwich and considered it before sinking her teeth into the crusty roll. Everything was riding on her first reaction to that bite. This was key. Anyone who didn't like

Robertos had no taste buds and needed to be loved harder for their handicap.

The Cubano crumbled as she took her first bite and her eyes rolled into the back of her head. "This..." she tried to talk and suddenly needed a deep drink of water. "Spicy. But sooo gooood." She drew out the 'o' as she finished chewing. He tore the sandwich in half and offered one piece to her.

"Alright," Maggie sighed and daubed her face with a napkin. "You're right. This is good."

Satisfied, Wakefield took a hearty bite of his own sandwich. All was right with the world. She liked his favorite meal. This got him thinking though, about what else she liked?

"Listen," Wakefield set his half down and turned to face her. "Tell me about...linen tablecloths and candles? Seriously."

"I was just teasing..." Maggie objected, she indicated the partial sandwich in her hand. "This is really amazing. I even like eating outside sometimes."

"No, I know, but...I'm not. Tomorrow night? There's a very fancy place in the next town I would love to take you to. If you're free, I mean."

She stopped chewing for a moment. If he wasn't mistaken her eyes positively lit up as she nodded. Remarkably, she looked almost shy for a moment. "I would like that, yes."

"Good." Wakefield suddenly had his appetite back. He pulled a fry from the container and bit into it, the salty crust crackling in his mouth. He covered the awkward silence with food, but he never really took his eyes off of her. She was lovely and vibrant, and she liked Robertos. It was all he could have hoped for.

"Your Grand Opening is still scheduled, right?"

She looked a bit surprised at the change of subject, but there was relief there too. The silence had been rather long and to get to a safer topic was likely as welcome to her as it was to him.

"Yes. Um...I mean, it's really sort of pointless in a way, I've been getting so many people already and we're not even officially open yet."

"I've noticed that your place is becoming a community center." He was teasing her, but she nodded solemnly.

"It really has, but it's not just that. I've been getting catering jobs too, lots of them. I had no idea the people in this town threw so many parties. And business meetings? There are people holding business meetings here."

Wakefield laughed. "We're not that small." He thought for a moment and amended, "Well, yes, we really are, but this town will still surprise you if you let it. Anyway, I am glad to hear that you're doing so well. Are you sure you can take the time to have dinner with me? You sound busy." Not that he wanted to talk her out of it, but if she was going to be worried about the business while they were on the date, it wouldn't be pleasant for either of them.

"No," she waved that off and nearly splattered BBQ sauce on him. "Sorry. No, I have Garrett. Without him, I would be buried alive, but he can handle the worst of the prep."

"Garrett." He was going to run that background check on Maggie's new assistant when he got a chance. So far, he'd been so wrapped up in the murder, he just hadn't had time. Truthfully, it bothered him that Garret just showed up out of the blue, right before a man was killed. There was no reason to suspect Garrett of murder. There was no connection he knew of to link the two men, but coincidences were suspicious by their very nature.

"What do you know about him, anyway?" He tried to make the question sound casual, even light. He was ready for her to become defensive, even cancel their time together, but she looked thoughtful and grabbed a fry.

"Not a whole lot. I mean, I did check his references. I called his former employer. They sang his praises and told me he could walk on water. It's a rather famous place, it even has a Michelin star, so he's got the experience. I mean, I know it's not much in the way of research and I don't know much about his personal life. Why?"

"Do you still want me to run that background check on him, just to be sure?"

"Now you're acting like a sheriff." She gave him a look. "Wait...is there a little bit of jealousy in there?" She peered into his eyes as if looking for something. "I think I might see a little right there." She pointed a finger at his left eye.

"Maggie, there is a dead man who was killed right after this Garrett came to work for you." He stopped her reply with both hands raised. "I know, I know, but it's not going to hurt anything for me to make some inquiries. I just...I want you to be safe. He's in your place, he's working under your name. I just want to be sure."

"Fine. I guess it can't hurt. And now you got me a little paranoid." She took a fry and grinned around it as she bit down. "But I think I liked it better when I thought you were jealous."

Wakefield concentrated on the last of the sandwich for a moment. "I'll check on him tomorrow. I mean, unless something comes up with Gertler."

"Yeah, how is that going?" She seemed to be relieved to change the topic too, despite her teasing.

Wakefield shrugged and crumpled the wrapper. "I sent the laptop out, it's getting a thorough investigation. Not much else to do yet except wait."

She thought for a moment and rose to take the trash to the can. "Nothing from the car?"

Wakefield groaned. "Sorry. That darn car. It's still there. The thing is stuck in mud up to the axel, *and* it has a flat tire. The rental company is supposed to come out with a tow, but it's not a high priority and meanwhile, it's sinking a little more every day it sits there. They wait too much longer and it's going to become a permanent part of the marsh."

"No fingerprints or..." She tossed the trash and sat next to him again.

"Sure. All Gertler's. As far as we can determine, no one else drove it but him." He shrugged and stood, offering his hand to her. "So, no help there. He apparently drove out there alone and was killed probably where he lay. You ready?"

At her nod, he rose and offered her his hand.

She took it with a smile, not because she needed help up, but because she wanted to. He could tell the difference and if he stood a little straighter because of it, maybe he could be forgiven his pride. Her hand felt good in his. Natural. He headed them back toward the bakery but didn't let go of her hand, and she didn't pull away. It was a grand feeling to say the least, even if they must have looked like kids on a first date.

On further reflection, that didn't seem like such a bad thing.

They walked a short distance in silence, content to be together. "Tomorrow night?" he asked when they arrived at her door.

"Tomorrow night. I'm getting dressed up, so no food trucks, no matter how tasty they might be. I might wear heels and everything." She glanced down at her sensible shoes in mock dismay and he snickered.

"You've tried the best of the trucks, now we'll try the best steak this side of the Mississippi. I think you're going to like it."

She nodded and for the first time since meeting her, Wakefield found himself tongue-tied. He just didn't know what to say. He stood there staring at her. She stood there staring at him. He moved maybe a half inch toward her, her head came up, lips angling towards his.

Or maybe not. He might have been imagining it. He wasn't sure, and as sure as anything, he wasn't about to make the first move when he didn't know if it's what she wanted. Her hand in his felt fine though and he drew her hand up, thinking to lay a kiss on the back of it. The way knights of old would or some other such nonsense. But his radio crackled at that moment. They broke apart awkwardly, her with an apology and a soft, "I shouldn't keep you."

"Yeah, I gotta go."

He stared at her again, then before he lost his nerve entirely, leaned in to press a kiss upon her cheek, so quick and light that he almost wondered if he'd done it at all.

Then spinning toward the curb, he made a beeline for his truck, while at the same time pressing the button to respond back to the static-filled call. "Sheriff Wakefield here. Whatcha got?"

He felt her eyes on him all the way down to the street, but never looked back, not even once, in case it would break the spell.

Chapter Twelve

M aggie's phone rang as she watched Wakefield walk away. She was still a little dazed by the kiss upon her cheek and unsure just what she felt about it. There was a certain giddiness that he had taken the initiative. At the same time, she couldn't help but wonder if things were moving a little too fast. It hadn't been all that long since she'd been engaged. Was she really ready for this?

With these thoughts racing through her mind, it was no wonder she answered her phone without looking first to see who it was.

"You're in, kid, if you want it."

Maggie drew the phone away from her face long enough to make sure it was her dad she was talking to. He seemed too upbeat. Giddy almost. "Dad?"

"I've got you in. Hurley. The man in the state prison an hour away? You're on the list, you and Mindy. If you want to go see him."

The change in direction from lunch date to murder investigation left Maggie somewhat at sea. It took her a minute to puzzle through what he'd just said. "We can visit the prison?"

"Isn't that what I just said?" he asked, clearly puzzled at her response.

Maggie laughed as she settled at one of the outdoor tables rather than go inside and risk this conversation being overheard. "No, that's great dad. Really great. Did you find out anything about why he's there?"

"Just it all seems pretty open and shut. The man had been embezzling funds from his own company. He was caught by the IRS and is now doing time. Straightforward. Honestly, I'm surprised they gave him the sentence they did. Apparently, he'd gotten belligerent in court and started raving about the IRS investigator setting him up. Made some threats. Next thing you know, he's in jail doing some serious time where normally some hefty fines would have probably sufficed. Maybe some community service or even probation."

"You mean you might have gotten him off, counselor?"

"I could have gotten him a reduced sentence at the very least. But he had chosen to represent himself, no doubt because he was just that sure he'd been set up. Probably thought the truth would come out in the trial."

"And the investigator he accused?"

"Gertler."

Maggie stared out at the empty space at the curb where the sheriff had been parked only a few minutes before. It was a shame he'd already gone as he probably would have been interested in this news.

Of course, she didn't know if this was news. A man who had been engaged in a criminal act had tried to deflect his crime onto the man accusing him. Wakefield had told her just a few minutes ago how terribly busy he'd been. The last thing she wanted to do was waste his time, especially when he was investigating something so serious as a murder.

"Say Dad, could waiting to tell the sheriff about any of this be seen as withholding evidence?"

There was a short pause as he considered this. "Does he have the laptop for himself?"

"Well, yes. It's being looked at right now."

"Then I would say no. You're not doing anything except exploring a lead he already has."

Maggie smiled. "Dad, I'm starting to think you must have been a heck of a lawyer."

He chuckled. "The DA rejoiced mightily when I retired. Just...if you get in trouble, I never met you."

Laughing, she hung up. In truth, she was starting to think that between her resentment of him when she was growing up, and how little he'd been home, especially after mom died, that she'd never really known him at all.

It was something to think about.

Maggie abandoned the outdoor table and headed inside the bakery to see what chaos Garrett had created this time. To her surprise, the place was fairly quiet with the exception of Mindy who exploded up off of the counter stool she was perched on and launched herself toward Maggie without warning.

"You've got to help me!"

"Mindy, the last time you asked me for help, I wound up in a murder investigation. One which is far from solved I might add."

"Not that. We need to talk about something else." Mindy gave a look at Garrett who was polishing the monstrosity which brewed all manner of coffee and hauled Maggie to the furthest booth from the counter as she could get.

Maggie stumbled along in her wake, wondering if laughing would be the wrong move right now, especially given the look Garrett was giving them.

At the same time, he was awfully interested in what they were doing. He'd been polishing the same bit of machinery since she came in.

"I was about to ask if you wanted to go to prison with me tomorrow, but now I'm not sure if that's the right question to lead with. Are you okay?"

"Prison?" Mindy stared at her with the same expression she'd seen on Benny's face when she'd tried to get the dog to play dead. "Who's in prison?"

"One of Gertler's previous clients. To say he was a little disgruntled over how his own audit with the IRS went would be an understatement."

Mindy's eyes lit up. "I'm in. Anything which would put the suspicion somewhere else. Only...he's not a suspect, is he? If he's in prison, he can't have murdered Gertler."

"Not unless he got someone else to do it."

"Can prisoners do that?" Mindy asked and Maggie shrugged.

"Maybe?"

"Prisoners can arrange a lot of things if they have the right connections," Garrett said suddenly from beside them. Maggie looked up in surprise as Garrett set two coffees on the table along with a plate of biscotti.

Biscotti weren't even on the menu.

"What?" The single word was not the question she meant to ask. What she really wanted to know was how much Garrett had overheard of this conversation, and why he'd been listening in the first place.

"Prisoners. Sorry, I didn't mean to be eavesdropping. I was bringing over some coffee for you and heard...anyway, I thought I would offer an answer since you seemed to be looking for one. Prisoners aren't supposed to be able to do anything. It's part of the whole prison thing. But they work out ways to tell those on the outside what they need. Codes. Carefully worded messages passed along from visitors to individuals on the outside. Happens all the time."

Maggie stared at him. "And you know this...how?"

"*Orange is the New Black. Oz. Shawshank Redemption.* Ok, a couple of those are kind of classic, but I mean it's used all the time in book and movie plots. I figure the writers have to draw on at least some facts. Stands to reason."

"Right. Thanks."

The woman watched as Garrett disappeared back into the kitchen.

"Creepy," Maggie muttered and glanced over at Mindy, surprised to see a different sort of expression on Mindy's face entirely. *Is she...smiling?*

"Hey, earth to Mindy..." Maggie waved her biscotti in front of Mindy until the other woman blinked and looked back at her.

"Sorry, was thinking."

"As I was saying, we're cleared to visit tomorrow morning. If you want to go."

"I'm in."

Was Maggie mistaken or was Mindy kind of hesitant in her reply? Of course, Maggie couldn't blame her. Going into a prison was kind of daunting. Unless something else was on her mind...

"Mindy? You wanted to talk to me about something?"

"Someone." Mindy had her coffee mug cupped between her palms as if she was cold. "Tag."

"Something new happened?" Maggie was thinking about the way the radio chirped when Brannigan...why does Brannigan not work for her? She couldn't seem to stop calling him Wakefield in her mind.

Whatever. When Wakefield was leaving.

"Just...Did I tell you he had to move back in with us?"

Maggie almost dropped her biscotti and she'd only just taken the first bite.

Amazing. How Garrett does it, I don't know. I think he's almost as good as me.

Almost.

She gulped coffee to clear the crumbs from her throat before speaking. "Are you back together?"

"No, not like that." Mindy waved off the very idea of it. "He's not sleeping well. Barely eating. I put him in the guest room finally thinking it might help. Especially with Bobby around. But he doesn't come out unless I force him to. I dragged him over here for lunch and then made up a whole thing about how I needed laundry detergent just to make him go across the street and buy some. He needs to get out, be with other people."

"And maybe needs a little less of you?" Maggie was sympathetic to her plight. Tag was a bit on the needy side right now. She'd seen that when he was in Sweet Escapes just the other day.

"I'd like my life back. I..." Mindy leaned in, dropping her voice to a whisper. "I have a date tomorrow night."

"Oh. My." Maggie stared at her. "Well, good for you!"

But Mindy didn't seem to hear her congratulations. Instead, she was staring out the window at the grocery store across the street.

No, she was staring at Tag who was standing just outside the grocery store across the street. He was holding a plastic container of laundry detergent with one hand, only he wasn't carrying it so much as he looked like he was about to clobber someone with it. Probably the old guy shouting at him in the middle of the parking lot.

Mindy was already scrambling for the door. Maggie pelted after her.

"Why don't you leave me alone!"

Mindy had been right. To Maggie's dismay, Tag wasn't looking like himself at all. His hair was lanky, falling into his eyes like he needed a haircut but hadn't had one in a while. He'd lost weight, his face lean, his complexion grey. His sunken eyes could only be from exhaustion. His complexion, an indicator of poor diet and stress.

The man who faced him down wore jeans and a flannel shirt. He had to be eighty and wasn't shy about sharing his opinions. He pointed a quavering finger at Tag and shouted for the entire world to hear, "They ought to arrest you and make everyone's life easier!"

Tag wavered on his feet. Mindy grabbed his arm to steady him, but he shook her off. "I said beat it. You can't slander me like this. Why I'll...I'll sic my lawyer on you, Sean. You're not going to get away with vandalizing my property. You're not going to get away with...whatever this is. I'm done, do you hear me? DONE."

Maggie winced. Her dad would love this.

Thankfully Sean didn't seem to be very comfortable with the crowd he was drawing. He muttered an imprecation, turned around and went back into the store. Tag just about crumbled, sagging heavily against Mindy.

"I can't do it. I can't sell out to Sean. I can't let him make me do it," he murmured, and Maggie moved in to support him from the other side. "He never saw the potential of Space Y. No one did."

"Back to Sweet Escapes?" Maggie asked Mindy quietly, appalled at the state Tag was in. "We could get some coffee into him. Some sugar maybe? It's good for shock."

Mindy shook her head. "I think I just want to get him home. Our car is over there." She pointed and Maggie nodded.

"Let's do this."

It took a little doing. Thankfully, Tag seemed to shake himself out of the daze he was in about halfway to the car. He made it the rest of the way without help. Mindy and Maggie watched him get into the car while they finalized their plans for the next day.

"Tomorrow morning, first thing," Maggie reminded her. "If you can leave him?"

"I'll figure something out." Mindy sighed switching the laundry detergent from one hand to the other. "Something's got to give. Tag needs his life back. We all do."

Chapter Thirteen

"Why does this feel a little like *Thelma and Louise*?" Mindy was practically singing as they escaped town in a little red convertible Maggie didn't even know she had until that morning.

"What?"

"You know, the old movie...two women on the run, facing things on their own terms. Nothing holding them back..."

Maggie gave her a sharp look. "The car sailing over a cliff with a million police cars chasing after them? Seriously Mindy, are you sure you're okay to drive?"

"It just feels good to get away. I mean...not to have to deal with that." Mindy slowed as they passed Doxie who was striding down the sidewalk with her trusty metal detector slung over her shoulder.

Maggie twisted in the seat to look behind them as the car continued on. Doxie clearly was going somewhere, though being at the edge of town like that it was hard to say just where. "What do you suppose she's up to? I mean, should we tell someone?"

"She's fine. There's nothing wrong with treasure hunting. It keeps her busy, and she seems happy enough."

Maggie settled back in her seat. "You were worried before..."

"Well, maybe now I'm not. There are worse things than digging up the yard. I mean look at us. We're going to the state prison!"

"There is that..."

Maybe Mindy was right. What they needed was a break, and with the town disappearing behind them, and the interstate just a few miles away, the day seemed full of possibility. Maybe this trip would answer a lot of questions, giving them what they needed to clear Tag, and move on with their lives. There had been far too much murder in Maggie's life since she'd come back home to stay. Maybe if things settled down, she could focus on the more normal issues in life.

Like what Mindy was up to later.

"So...date tonight?" she asked, but Mindy only laughed and turned up the radio, which led to them bickering over which station to listen to.

Yep. There was a lot to be said for normalcy.

Maggie might have, sorta on purpose, neglected to tell Mindy the circumstances which got them into the prison.

"What all was written on those documents we presented when we came in? We work for your dad?" she asked when they had a moment alone together after going through a whole set of questions and verifications. This got them as far as a waiting room, just outside the actual visitation area.

Maggie winced. Maybe she should have explained this beforehand, but she'd been worried Mindy wouldn't have agreed to coming, if she'd known. "It's hard to get in to see someone when you're not on their list of friends and acquaintances. Legal teams are much easier. We're listed as interns."

"Your father is retired. What office?"

"Not entirely retired. He's Tag's lawyer."

"That's so much better. Look," she hissed the words in Maggie's ear, absolutely furious. "Could we get arrested for this? Because I think Bobby having one parent in jail at a time is about enough, don't you?"

"Tag isn't in jail, and he's not going to be!"

"That doesn't mean I won't be, before the end of the day. I have a—"

"Date, yes, I know. And you still won't tell me who you're seeing. Now hush, apparently, they're letting us in." Maggie pushed her away with a roll of her eyes and followed the guard who escorted them into a large room, which reminded Maggie somewhat of a school cafeteria. The space was dotted with tables, and they were instructed where they were to sit and wait. They weren't the only ones there. Several other individuals filtered in with them, each taking their assigned places quietly.

Maggie couldn't get over how quiet it was. How sad. There were a lot of grim expressions, shoulders slumped in resignation. Pain.

Then the inmates came in and everything changed. Around them the other visitors brightened, Maggie saw hope, even joy in each face when they first saw their loved one. It was obvious that while this wasn't where their families wanted to see them, they were soaking in the reassurance that came of seeing their family member unharmed. Alive. Safe. Knowing they made it through another week had to be worth a lot.

In the meantime, they waited, watching the door for someone who looked like the grainy picture Maggie had of Hurley Watkins. She reminded herself that he should be kind of thin and reedy, with a head of sandy colored hair and slightly confused...no stunned...expression of disbelief on his face. At least that was what the picture taken at his hearing had looked like. He was probably less confused and more angry now.

Well, she was at least part right.

What they got was a bald man with bulging biceps and a hardened expression. He sat down across from them, arms crossed, angry and defiant. "More lawyers. Alright, let's get this over with."

It's him. Maggie saw it in the shape of his face, somewhere in the eyes. Hurley had changed in prison and he's no longer the kid he was when he went in.

Maggie's idea that he might be somehow behind Gertler's murder, suddenly didn't seem quite so far-fetched.

She cleared her throat and began. "Mr. Watkins, my name is—"

"Look, if I wanted a social call, I would have said so. You got fifteen minutes, and if you're here to help get me out, don't waste my time with small talk. Let's get on with it, alright?"

To Maggie's surprise, Mindy is right there, stepping into the conversation as smoothly as if she'd done this kind of interrogation a thousand times. "Exactly. Thank you, Mr. Watkins. Why don't we start with how much Mr. Gertler asked for when he told you he would make the charges go away, and how much you actually gave him."

Hurley stared at her. Maggie stared at her.

Who is this woman?

This version of Mindy is hard as nails. Her eyes glittered with the sort of determination Maggie dimly remembered from back when Mindy was running for homecoming queen. In high school, she had been a girl who always got what she wanted. Maggie saw traces of that girl now in this woman, and she had to admit she admired her for it. Mindy had been beaten down so long by the circumstances around her, that for a period of time, that version of Mindy had kind of gotten lost.

No more.

Hurley seemed to like what he saw as well because a slow smile formed as he looked her up and down, nodding with a certain grudging respect. "I like you. Alright. Let's get on with it."

For the next fifteen minutes he gave them details, a lot of them. They weren't allowed to bring in any types of devices for recording the conversation, but they were allowed to take notes by hand. Since Mindy is building a decent rapport with the guy, Maggie was the one scribbling, pausing, sometimes to clarify details.

Numbers. Dates. How he'd gotten the money and how he paid it. He gave them everything, and Maggie didn't doubt a word of it. Hurley softened toward the end of his interview as he seemed to realize this too.

"You actually believe me."

"We do."

"That I'd paid him off and he got me arrested anyway?"

"Every word of it," Mindy said softly. "Because he did it to others. The extortion. Recently."

Hurley sat back and stared at her. "That's what this is about? You're building a case to put him away? I've got news for you. That kind of evil doesn't belong in a jail cell. I'd kill him if I could."

Maggie and Mindy exchanged glances.

"Mr. Watkins," Maggie set down her pencil and looked at him, really looked at him. "Gertler is dead. He was murdered."

He reared back as if struck.

"Wait. What? Are you saying you came here to see if I did it somehow? If I ARRANGED it? Are you kidding? You're not content to pin one thing on me but you're going to pin something else? You think you can keep me here forever?"

He'd risen up in this dialogue. Shouting the last words. Furious. Violent. Terrifying.

Maggie and Mindy jumped up as well, backing away as far from every corner of the room the guards descended. Hurley was still shouting threats and imprecations as he was hustled out one door, his voice growing fainter even if his fury wasn't. Maggie barely even noticed as they were shoved out of the room, and back to the lockers. They were told quietly and without fanfare that they would need to gather their things and go.

Just like that their visit was over. They hadn't even been able to grab their notes from the table before leaving.

To make matters worse, Mindy wasn't even speaking to her. She appeared shaken, her hand fumbling with the locker, like she couldn't get it open. In fact, she was so rattled she was crying, and she couldn't seem to get the code to work so she could remove her purse and go.

"Let me help." Maggie went to the counter and explained to the woman at the desk what the problem was. The woman sighed and came around to help.

Through the plexiglass, Maggie could just make out one of the computer screens of many, which made up the array the woman had been looking at. If she craned her neck just so, she could make out the log on the screen, listing off expected visitors and appointment times. One name in particular stood out.

Sheriff Brannigan Wakefield was due to talk to Hurley Watkins within the hour.

"Well, crud," she muttered and turned back in time to see Mindy wrench the door to her locker open. Maggie bolted across the room, grabbing her purse for her. Her stomach felt like they were sailing over a cliff in a convertible. "We need to leave," she whisper-shouted, practically towing Mindy from the room. "Now!"

Chapter Fourteen

It's not easy being angry at someone who knocks your socks off when they enter a room. Maggie was wearing a little black dress that set her figure off and she had done her hair in a way he hadn't seen before. It looked nice, with little tendrils dancing about her ears with the rest upswept in a way which made her appear more elegant and refined somehow. Too good for the likes of him. Her shoes though looked horribly uncomfortable, even if they were beautiful in how they set off her legs.

Wakefield had been schooling himself all day to hold onto the anger. For her sake, not his. Being confronted with a goddess wasn't part of the plan.

As she walked to the table, many heads turned at the restaurant, appreciative stares and no small curiosity to see who it was that merited a dinner with such a lovely woman. The fact that she glided across the room, making walking on those heels seem effortless only added to the illusion of perfection. He swallowed hard, standing up naturally to greet her. She couldn't have known what he did, or she never would have allowed him to seat her in a very old-fashioned manner which would have normally been enough to make him burst with pride.

Normally.

"I am sorry I had to meet you here," she started as he sat. "I've been swamped with prepping for the Grand Opening, and I had to run home and change at the last minute. Thank you for understanding."

He took the cloth napkin and draped it over his lap in silence. He took a moment to smooth it out while he contemplated the right words to bring the conversation around to what needed to be said. Especially when what he wanted was to scream at her for several minutes, accusing her of foolishness and frivolity. Of course, that would have set a poor tone for their date.

"So...how was your day?" She prompted as the silence between them lengthened. She was frowning now, watching his face carefully, as if sensing something was wrong.

"I too had a busy day." He looked into her eyes. "You see, I had asked to be notified when anyone went to see Hurley." She paled, her eyes growing wider. "Yes. Can you imagine how surprised I was when two women applied to speak to him? Two *women* visiting a men's maximum security prison?"

She took her turn now in arranging her napkin carefully on her lap. "I was briefed on the protocols and even what to wear." Her voice was steady. How could she be so resolute and without any apparent guilt?

"Hurley had to be restrained. Put into solitary to cool down for a bit," Wakefield told her. He waved away the waiter as he approached. "He was too...upset for me to question him today. Apparently, he thinks you and Mindy are trying to set him up for murdering Gertler."

Maggie winced. "That's nonsense." She made a grab for her glass of ice water but didn't drink. "I never said..."

"Maggie, that isn't the point. Why...why did you two even go there? And why would your father, of all people sanction this, even help you get in?"

"Because he thinks I'm an adult?" She gulped her drink, setting the glass down hard enough to send water sloshing over the side of the glass.

He was on dangerous ground. If he pushed her too hard, not only could he lose her, but he could lose any chance of keeping her safe. She was likely to jump in headfirst into some cockamamy scheme and get her and Mindy both killed. He forced himself to be calm and tried again.

"Just...tell me why you wanted to talk to Hurley."

"I...*we* thought maybe it was possible that he could have wanted revenge on Gertler. He blames him for the prison sentence and claims that..."

"He had an airtight alibi. A few dozen guards and a couple hundred prisoners can vouch for his whereabouts for the past few years."

"But, in the movies, there's always a way to get a message out or hire someone, or..."

"This *isn't* a movie. This is real and it has very real and very permanent consequences. Two attractive women in that place can be a real problem, not to mention that if there was any involvement by Hurley, he has now been warned that someone is on to him."

"That he could have done it? Or had it done?"

Wakefield took a breath, debating the merit of answering. "Yes, he has gotten things, comfort things smuggled in for himself. Cigarettes. Chocolate. Magazines. That is *very* different from arranging someone's murder."

"Ok, but listen." Maggie leaned over the table, her eyes intent on his. "I did get information that you need to know. Don't condemn me until you hear." She paused until he nodded. "Alright. He *did* bribe Gertler. He confessed to that. Gertler apparently took the bribe and still sent Hurley away."

"He confessed to it?"

"Yes." Maggie nodded fiercely.

"How did you know to ask him about bribes?" Maggie sat back a little and seemed to freeze. Wakefield stifled a groan. "You had information about someone else taking a bribe? Or giving one to Gertler? Who? Tag? What have you been keeping from me, Maggie?"

She sat back and dropped her eyes to the napkin again. Wakefield couldn't stop the groan that escaped his lips. "Maggie...just because an inmate is able to finagle a way to get things in prison, that is a far cry from putting a hit out on another person. Not every prisoner is connected to some mysterious mafia that kills on command."

"I know that."

"I don't think you do." He took a moment to think through what he needed to say. "I'm worried. You're messing with some very dangerous areas. Someone has already been killed. You'd do well to remember that. Someone out there has already PROVEN they would take a life if it suits their needs. If you get too close, there's no reason to think they wouldn't kill again. Please. Stay out of this. Let me handle it." He reached over to squeeze her hand. "I really am good at my job."

"I know you are..." she said it so quietly she wasn't sure he'd heard her.

"I just don't want you to get hurt, or Mindy either. I may not personally like Taggart, but that isn't going to cloud my judgement. I *am* looking into this whole matter. I'm even conducting a full investigation – by the book."

"I know...but this...Gertler..." Maggie drew back her hand, setting it in her lap, "Well, he's dead...murdered and everyone who knew him suddenly wants to throw a party. This isn't the devil, it was a man, a human being and no one seems to care. Even Mindy is only wanting to clear Tag's name. It's just wrong for someone to die and be...despised even in death. It's just wrong."

"I get it, but I don't have any opinion of the man, alive or not. I'm not letting his character get in the way of the investigation either. I will find out what happened to him."

"Of course, I trust you..."

"But that's part of the problem, isn't it?"

"That I trust you?"

"That you trust *everyone*. Yes, you can trust me, but then I hope that I've earned your trust by now. But sometimes you're a little...please don't take offense...quick to give that trust to those around you. You really need to be more careful with your friends."

"What do you mean?" Maggie cast him a confused look. "Is this about Garrett again?"

"Well, there is that. But I mean...well, like that woman you're becoming friends with."

"Mindy?" She nearly laughed. "You've known Mindy for a long time too..."

"No." Wakefield shook his head, "I mean this Janet person."

"Janet? I've known her since we were kids. She went to high school with me, here in our town. Most folks around here remember Janet."

"Maybe, but she's not a teenager anymore. And those good folks who remember her are suddenly not so happy to see her. Did you know that she is going around the town asking for money?"

"Money? Why? I thought she was doing great. She's always so put together. The shoes she was wearing the other day cost more than my entire outfit I'm wearing right now." He must have been staring at her because she blushed suddenly. "Not that I bought everything new to wear just for tonight or anything."

He snorted. "Just...keep in mind Janet tells different stories depending on her audience. I've had more than one complaint that she's been making the rounds of all her old friends saying she's trying to leave her husband, but she doesn't have the funds to get out on her own. She has a whole sob story about how she needs the money so she can start over."

"That doesn't sound like her..." Maggie said to her herself. "She was telling me about her import business and the whole internet thing..."

"That's a mark of a good con." He held up a hand when she started to say something. "I know you don't want her to be lying, but her story is slick and polished. Then she comes to you and says that life is all roses and fine wine. All I'm saying is be careful. She will likely hit you up soon for money and it won't be a small sum. Leaving her abusive husband or needing someone to buy stock in her internet company or...what did you say? Imports?"

"I can't believe she would..."

"How long has it been since you've seen her? People change. I hope I'm wrong, but I am hearing from several people now that have been having second thoughts after giving her money to help her out. All in large amounts of cash."

But Maggie was shaking her head. "I really don't believe it. Janet happens to be a friend of mine. I mean, she's already helped get the bakery on the map. I mean the internet map. She's never asked for a dime for all of that. I'm sure there's been some misunderstanding..."

He was losing her again. Between insulting her friend and trying to warn her against going off half-cocked on the wild do-it-yourself investigation, she was defensive and getting angry again. Having said his piece, his anger had faded, but it appeared that it transferred to her.

He took a long breath and started to say that they could work out whatever differences they had, or maybe to change the topic. He could even suggest that they order. That waiter was certainly hovering long enough, but at that moment his phone rang.

He sighed and fished the infernal device from his pocket. "Yes?"

"Sheriff, sorry to bother you, but we have a situation here. We got a fire out at the Werther place, it's getting bad. Real bad. They're calling in a MABAS box."

Wakefield swore. "I'm on the way." He reached into his pocket and pulled out his wallet. "Maggie, I have to go, there's a fire and I need to get there. They're calling a MABAS..." he shook his head and pulled a credit card from his wallet and set it on the table. "Mutual Aid Box Alarm System. It means that fire fighters and emergency vehicles are coming from everywhere. I have to go."

"Maybe I should go too? I might be able to help somehow..."

"Maggie, have you been listening to a word I've been saying?" He jumped to his feet, gesturing at the card he'd left on the table. "Have dinner on me. Order what you want. I'll see you later." He paused a moment and bent to kiss her cheek. He thought to try her lips, but under the circumstances, she still seemed to not like him at the moment, and he had no time to stay and smooth things over.

It really was a shame. As he passed by other tables on the way out, he caught a glimpse of what the other diners were eating. It looked like it would have been a good dinner.

Chapter Fifteen

Well, that certainly hadn't gone well.

Maggie stared a long time at the menu still sitting on the table in front of her. She wasn't exactly hungry, but she was mad enough to order a nice dinner for herself anyway. Worst case scenario, she wouldn't wind up eating a bite of it and Benny would get a fairly nice doggie bag out of the deal.

The waiter, if anything, was sympathetic.

"Not a pleasant evening, no?" he asked in a thick French accent. "But he pays for dinner so..." he shrugged but she could detect the wicked glint in his eye.

She laughed. "What do you recommend?"

"Tell me your feelings on lobster..."

In the end, Maggie wasn't quite as vengeful as all that, though, she did order a steak and the sommelier was able to pair it with a very nice wine. Not that Maggie needed to order the entire bottle, but right now she was in a bit of a mood, and it certainly helped to take the edge off.

"So, I get a rideshare home later. I went to a prison today and then my boyfriend up and throws all these conspiracies at me as if I'm not able to see for myself when someone is lying to me."

"*Mais oui*, but I would do the same if I had a day like yours," the server responded, and Maggie hadn't realized she'd spoken out loud.

"I should not have said all that," she murmured, eyeing her glass which seemed to never be quite empty.

"You are talking about that horrible Mr. Gertler though, are you not? The man who died who was so unpleasant." The waiter removed her salad plate deftly, sliding the next course before her. She didn't even remember eating it, though the plate he removed was empty.

She stared at her soup a bit nonplussed. When had she ordered soup? "Was he unpleasant? I only saw him once in the street."

The waiter made a face. "He would only eat here when he was in town. A man such as he, has expensive taste, no? I saw him the night before he died." The man made a wry face. "He got into a fight too. Picked a fight with a stranger at the bar."

"A stranger? How do you know they didn't know each other?"

"This particular gentleman was definitely a stranger. He was picking up an order. Had a nice simple name to remember, so short. Lee. I would remember a Lee."

Lee.

Garrett Lee, who came in to work with a black eye the morning Gertler's body was found.

"Can you..." She couldn't breathe. It all just made so much sense...and no sense at all. "Can you please have my dinner wrapped. To go. I suddenly don't feel well."

"Of course." The waiter's tone was uncertain. Likely worrying that he was the cause of her upset and that it would somehow translate to the tip. Maggie shook her head. Whatever. It wasn't important. Right now, what she needed more than ever was to get in touch with Wakefield and let him know what she'd found out.

Except he was at that fire. Or on his way to it. And she only had a supposition. A theory. Gertler was an unpleasant man. He might easily have just picked a fight with a stranger. Garrett had been in the wrong place at the wrong time.

Except he'd been lying to her. At the very least by omission. Hadn't he?

Suddenly she wasn't sure just what he'd said and hadn't said. Times like this she really wished she could somehow rewind her life just so she could go back and hear conversations over again. The problem was, she'd had a glass of wine or two and wasn't remembering anything quite clearly.

Like right now. She'd pulled out her phone in the last few minutes but had no idea who to call.

In the meantime, the hostess was trying to seat a guest who clearly had no desire to take another step across the dining room once he caught sight of Maggie.

"You."

Maggie winced. This man she remembered. She'd last seen him in the street, outside the grocery store. "Sean McClellen, isn't it?" she asked with a bright smile that dimmed when the man came toward her pointer finger out. He brandished it like a weapon in her direction, only just coming up short from poking her outright.

"You were with that no-good rascal the other day."

"Tag? Well, he has his moments."

"He's a scoundrel, a fraud, and a murderer."

Maggie paused. She wasn't one to get into fights. Maybe what came next could be blamed on the wine, or perhaps on the fact that her assistant had betrayed her, or even the dressing down she'd gotten from the high and mighty Brannigan Wakefield. Either way, she wasn't taking any of this sitting down anymore.

Maggie rose up until she was about nose to nose with the old coot. "If you like calling names so much maybe we should add in a few of your own. Vandal maybe? Are you the one damaging Tag's place? Busybody? Or maybe you like throwing about the word 'murderer' to cover your own evil intentions. Where were you the night Gertler was killed? What were you doing?"

McClellen sputtered a bit. Apparently, her fighting back hadn't occurred to him and now he was aware of the other diners staring. His gaze darted around the room, and she guessed he was seeing the same things she was. The curious gazes. The growing discontent that their fine dining experience was being spoiled.

"No answer?" she asked, irritated that he'd gotten tongue tied when he'd been liberal enough with his comments only a few minutes ago. "Nothing you'd like to go on the record saying?"

"Never you mind what I was up to. It has nothing to do with you." With that he spun on his heel and stormed out of the place.

Which left Maggie standing in the middle of a restaurant which had gone completely silent. Even the string quartet was no longer playing. "Well," she said as she saw her waiter returning with a large bag which she supposed held her dinner. "How about this. Dessert is on me tonight. Crème Brule all around!" With that she handed Wakefield's card to the manager and smiled. "You can put it on this."

Chapter Sixteen

Maggie hardly slept at all that night, her mind just would not let her rest. Between everything that had happened in the last few days - the frustration of her fight with Brannigan, and the revelations about her new assistant - it was a wonder she slept at all.

She woke groggy, with the beginnings of a migraine long before the sun came up. She used the time wisely though, going in early to the bakery and getting started on the day's baking.

It felt good to be working dough again. This last week, she really hadn't been spending enough time in the kitchen. As she measured and stirred, a sort of peace came over her. Whatever else happened today, she still had this, here. She loved what she was creating with Sweet Escapes and really was looking forward to the official opening.

So caught up frosting a batch of cupcakes for a church luncheon, she almost didn't hear Garrett come in. She sensed him though, his consternation and surprise at finding her doing the task she'd told him was his to manage yesterday.

"I take it that you already know?" he said finally, and when she looked up, she saw something on his face which surprised her. Not anger or remorse, but resignation. Regret.

"That you argued with Gertler, yes." She straightened and wiped her hands on a towel. "Care to explain?"

Whatever he'd expected her to say, it hadn't been that. He recoiled slightly, a stiffening of his shoulders telling her she'd hit on something he hadn't anticipated her to find out.

Just who was he anyway?

"I don't know what you're talking about." He reached for a mixing bowl and started measuring out flour with a practiced hand.

"You know exactly what I'm talking about. That little bald man you confronted in the supper club last week. That? There were *witnesses*, Garrett."

Garrett stared at her for a moment and laughed. He actually laughed so hard that he had to set down the measuring cup he was using.

Of all the responses he could have had, Maggie hadn't imagined this. "Are you kidding me?" she asked, piqued that he was treating this so lightly. "The man turned up DEAD the VERY NEXT DAY."

"It was about his *car*. Some stranger came up to me and claimed I'd scratched his car in the parking lot. Guy was three sheets to the wind or something. Look, you've got to believe me, I'd never even heard of a Gertler before last week. And while the guy was a legitimate jerk, I certainly didn't kill him if that's what you're thinking." Still chuckling, he resumed measuring out flour.

Maggie stared at him. "Right. Um...sorry. Just...carry on. You're starting on the pastries for the opening?"

Still stiff and awkward, Maggie gave some terse instructions, finished off the last of the cupcakes and went to wash her hands. What could she do but watch him? Garrett had already braced for her to be confronting him about something else, that much was clear. If it wasn't about Gertler, then what? She was starting to wish she'd done that background check after all.

The rest of the morning passed in a flurry of activity. Sweet Escapes opened, and Maggie was delighted to see a lot of returning customers. People were getting used to coming in, which boded well for business. Maybe her little bakery and coffee shop would make a success after all.

She was taking an order at one of the tables when Mindy came in. Maggie started to call to her but stopped when she saw how Mindy made a beeline for the counter. Garrett was just setting out a fresh supply of cookies in the case and paused in what he was doing to greet her.

It was Mindy's reaction which really threw her.

Mindy leaned on the case as she talked, smiling and twirling her hair with one finger.

Twirling her hair!

Many things came clear in that instant. Garrett's return smile, the way he teased her and made her laugh. Mindy's mystery date had very likely been with Maggie's suspicious pastry chef. Maggie finished taking the order, sure she had probably muddled it in her distracted state and headed straight for the counter.

"Hey Mindy! I was hoping you'd stop by!"

She spoke brightly, shooting Garrett a look which sent him back to the kitchen, but not before leaning in to kiss Mindy on the cheek.

Wide-eyed now, Maggie hauled Mindy aside.

"How long has this been going on? And what do you know about him anyway?"

She tried to ask the questions in a chatty way, but it came out through clenched teeth. There were far too many secrets around here this morning and she didn't like being in the dark. But Mindy only giggled and looking past Maggie, shouted a hello to Tag, who'd just walked in.

Frustrated now, Maggie found a smile to greet him with, knowing he probably needed the encouragement. Except he was genuinely happy, waving papers as he approached, talking a million miles an hour about something to do with Space Y and a ComSat deal, which made no sense at all.

Mindy and Maggie looked at each other, and immediately dragged him over to a table.

"You're going to explain," Maggie said firmly as she sat him down. "As soon as I put this order in."

She hurried into the kitchen, colliding with Garrett who was just coming out. There was much confusion for a moment as they righted themselves.

"I saw Tag and I came out to give you a break so you could talk," he said, and she glanced at him in surprise.

"Then take care of this." She put her order pad into his hand and returned to the table where her friends waited. "What did I miss?"

"Some kind of deal?" Mindy said, her expression showing she knew as little about this as Maggie did.

"It's a ComSat deal...it means we won't be putting passengers into space, but objects. Satellites. I've been on the phone all morning about this. In fact..." He held up his cell phone which was ringing, and pushed the button to answer, stepping out of the restaurant to do so.

Mindy and Maggie watched him go. When Maggie spoke, it was in an awed whisper. "Did that say—"

"Richter Eberhart?"

"Tech Billionaire Richter Eberhart? Owns his own space station, Richter Eberhart? Yes. I believe it did."

Through the front door of the window, they could see Tag outside jumping up and down fist pumping. Muffled shouts could be heard through the glass.

A moment later he came back in.

"You're going to explain what this is all about, Tag!" Mindy said the moment he was within range. "Get over here this instant! How do you know Richter Eberhart?"

"I met him through an event my college sponsored. He was the guest speaker, and I had a chance to talk to him a few minutes afterwards. It wasn't long after I finished my engineering degree and started my Masters—"

"Hang on, you finished your degree?"

Mindy's expression was one of pure astonishment. Tag was blushing and smiling in a shy, but proud way. "I've been doing most of the classes online. I kind of pushed to finish in the last few weeks. With everything that happened, it was good to have something to concentrate on. Anyway, I need to go. I really only have time for coffee and maybe a couple of those cinnamon rolls?"

"Huh? Yes, of course. Tag, I should have asked you when you came in. Mindy, did you need anything?"

Mindy was still sitting there, her eyes blank. She shook herself out of her daze. "Nothing, thanks."

Maggie bustled about getting his order. When she came back to the table, Mindy had recovered herself somewhat, and was even smiling for the first time in days. In fact, they both seemed so relaxed, Maggie felt comfortable enough to ask a question that had been pressing for a while now.

"Before you go, Tag, and if you have a second Mindy, I was wondering something. Did either of you know Gertler in high school?"

Tag shrugged. "Kind of? He was a couple years younger than us, but he was at all the games."

Mindy laughed. "I remember that. Little snot. Hated being there but his parents dragged him because his sister was a cheerleader. A sophomore when we were seniors, so I suppose you wouldn't remember her, Maggie."

"Sister?" Maggie tried to remember, but Mindy had been right. She really was drawing a blank. She'd just never paid enough attention to cheerleaders back then.

"Sara. She married a few years back. I think she became a Monroe or something. Tag, do you remember?"

He shrugged. "Not a clue. Though I remember Sara. Cute. Flirted a lot."

Mindy punched him in the arm. "Only because you were the star quarterback. Every girl flirted with you a lot."

Tag was grinning. "Hey, when you've got it, you've got it. Ouch! Okay, I'm sorry!"

Maggie ignored them, busy thinking through this new information. "Shouldn't she have showed up here or something when her brother died? Or his parents or something?"

"Sara's parents died about a year after we graduated. I remember because it was a pretty bad accident. They put in the stop light over on 3rd after it happened. Too little, too late, you know? Life seems to be like that. Someone has to die before anything changes."

With that she grabbed her purse and the cup of coffee Maggie had brought over for her. "Sorry, Mags. I'm going to run. I want to hear more about Tag's noble project. See you later!"

"No problem. Thanks, guys." Maggie watched them go with an absent smile.

Something niggled at the back of her mind. Something she should have noticed in that conversation which she hadn't. Shaking her head, she turned away. There were cookies to bake still for the opening. If she didn't start now, she'd never finish.

Chapter Seventeen

Maggie couldn't get it out of her head. Gertler's sister. Sara Gertler. Married and had become a Monroe. Or something like a Monroe.

She was missing something. What was she missing?

Sara. Sara Gertler.

Try as she might, she couldn't remember her. Had the girl had a nickname perhaps? Something else?

Sadie. Sadie was a nickname for Sara. Monroe. Montrose. She'd never followed up on that particular clue and regretted it soundly. A search using her phone helped her to find Sadie on social media. Pictures showed her working at a dress shop a couple of towns over.

But what did she have? If Sadie Montrose really was Gertler's sister, then her brother coming after her husband for a tax thing could be motive, especially if her husband wound up dead because of it. But means? Or even ability? Gertler had been killed with an arrow. How many people knew how to shoot a bow with that level of ability?

When she finished with her tasks for the day, Maggie told Garrett to clean up and just about ran back to her father's house, something Benny didn't mind. The dog hadn't been getting much attention lately, and he enjoyed romping alongside her.

Maggie and Benny took the stairs two at a time into the house. She headed straight for her old bedroom, which was too cluttered. She'd brought home too much stuff from her old city life when she'd returned. Added to the ephemera from her childhood, it was a wonder sometimes she could find anything at all.

It was her childhood memories she needed most right now. She knelt on the carpet and dug around in the bookshelf across from her bed. With a wild shout of triumph she dove, pulling out the blue and silver hardcover from the bottom shelf.

Her high school yearbook was just as she'd remembered it, full of well wishes and scribbled messages, most of which made no sense now. Another time it might have been amusing to see what was written there. Right now though she was more interested in the index, and the list of page numbers next to each name showing where she could find them.

Sara Gertler was listed in four places. The first was her sophomore picture and showed a smiling girl with dark curly hair and brown eyes. The next page was a team photo with the cheerleading squad. Mindy stood two cheerleaders over, smiling broadly for the camera. Maggie paused on this picture picking out other names and faces she knew. Janet was there as well, looking somewhat morose, her smile strained. Maggie wondered what had been bothering her old friend back then to make her look so sad.

Shaking her head, she moved on to the next picture, which was of the homecoming dance. Sara was part of the homecoming court, not the queen, though the fact that she was representing her class was impressive.

It was the fourth picture though which got her attention. Maggie gasped when she saw the heading on the page – the Archery Club.

Sara knew very well how to handle a bow, the very instrument used to take her brother's life.

"It's nothing. Circumstantial."

"What's circumstantial?" Her father was passing by her door, still dressed for his day at the golf course. Maggie looked up in surprise. She hadn't heard him come in.

"This." She waved the book at him until he took it. She quickly explained her suspicions and what she had found. "I mean the fact that she knows how to shoot shouldn't mean anything, right? I mean there's about thirty kids here. I know most of them. Archery was a popular sport. She's standing right there next to Janet and a couple of other girls like they were all friends. They might have gone out together to get some kind of gym credit or something. It doesn't mean she was any good at it."

Her father studied the picture, a frown deepening on his brow. "Do you know where she is now?"

"I know where she works. I thought...well maybe I could try questioning her at work. It'd be less dangerous that way."

Her father handed back the book. "Even less so if you have company."

She gave him a quick look. "You'll come?"

"Try and keep me away. Besides, you're going to need me if you want to learn proper questioning technique."

Maggie laughed. "And to keep from getting arrested. Only...go change first. I can't believe men still wear checkered pants on the golf course."

***

It took half an hour to reach the store where Sadie Montrose worked. She had changed quite a bit since high school, and if Maggie hadn't looked her up on social media first, she might have walked by her without recognizing her. Her hair was streaked purple now, her clothing more flamboyant, full of animal patterns and creative textures. Her left arm told a whole story in tattoos. The right held a portrait of her parents.

Maggie watched her wait on a customer with expertise and a definite level of salesmanship as she flattered the customer until they bought not only the sweater they'd come in for, but three more of the same garments in different colors.

With a look at her father who only shrugged, Maggie waited until Sadie was done ringing up her customer before approaching and introducing herself.

Sadie was wary, barely acknowledging the introduction. "I know who you are. My *dear* brother-in-law told me you might come sniffing around."

This surprised Maggie because she hadn't thought there was any love lost between the two, but at least it saved time on having to explain.

"I am sorry for your loss," she said, and caught herself. "Both of them."

"Don't be. Not on that no-good brother of mine. He deserved whatever happened to him. I lost the love of my life. My husband *committed suicide* because of him. My own brother, trying to extort money from him and when he couldn't pay, throwing him to the wolves? Can you imagine what I've been through? Nearly lost this place too. My husband's legacy. His pride and joy." She waved a hand broadly to indicate the store.

Maggie glanced quickly at her father, unsure how to proceed.

"Can you tell me where you were on the night your brother died?" he asked, interrupting smoothly. Or not so smoothly, but at least taking over the questioning where Maggie was floundering.

"I don't mind in the least. I was in New York on a buying trip, and you can verify that any of a dozen ways. Now if you'll excuse me, I have a business to run." With that she headed toward a customer who was fingering several blouses near the back of the store.

Well, that was that. Not exactly helpful but enlightening all the same.

"It's all fake." The statement came from a girl who looked no older than sixteen who had only just come out of the back room carrying several hangers with various items of clothing on them. She plopped them on the counter and reached for a price gun. She snapped clearance tags on each with a practiced hand. "All of it. She's lying about everything."

"Excuse me?" Maggie shot a quick glance at Sadie who was talking to the customer but glancing their way. Maggie grabbed at one of the shirts, a garish purple thing with sequins and held it up as if delighted in the find. "What do you mean?"

"She hated her husband. Was separated from him for months. I don't think she saw Sid face to face once in the last year."

Sadie was returning. Maggie thrust the shirt at the girl. "I don't think it's my size. Thank you."

With that she fled the store, practically dragging her father with her. "I don't get it," she said as they got in the car. "Was this a clue or a dead end?"

"A little of each. If anything, we understand why Gil Montrose wasn't too fond of Sadie."

Maggie paused, her hand hovering over the start button for the car and stared at him. "You lost me."

"Gil said any money from Sid's estate should have been his. He might actually have a case. If Sid had been legally separated from his wife, she might not actually be eligible to inherit his belongings, which in all likelihood, includes the ownership of that store. It's murky though and I wouldn't know without reading the terms of the will."

"So her pretending they were still together makes everything hers automatically then?"

Her father shrugged. "As I said, I'd need to see the terms of the will."

"Or if there even was a will..." Maggie murmured.

"Exactly. If there wasn't, then she might inherit automatically – so long as they were still married at the time of his death."

"Wow." Maggie started the car and put it into gear. "So, is she a suspect or not?"

An incoming call from Tag prevented further discussion. With more dismay than was probably warranted, Maggie answered, putting the call on her car's speaker system. "What's up, Tag? More billionaires vying for your attention?"

Tag was thankfully in a good enough mood that he didn't take offense by the comment. He only laughed. "Nothing quite so thrilling. I was hoping to get a favor."

"A favor?" Given that she was already trying to prove him innocent of murder, her plate was already full. Of course, he was also a friend...of sorts. "What do you need?"

"I just got a call from the rental company. They're coming out to tow Gertler's car. Because there's still an ongoing investigation, I'm not allowed on the property. I'm not comfortable with someone just going out there and doing whatever they like without anyone there to keep an eye on things. Not with the whole Space Y thing coming together the way it is. I haven't been able to reach Mindy, otherwise I'd never ask, not when you've been doing so much already..."

"You want me to babysit the guy with the tow truck?"

"Something like that."

Maggie glanced over at her father. "Up for a stop?"

"They're coming now?" he asked.

"Unfortunately, yes."

"I'm up for it if you are," he said and Maggie stifled a giggle at the expression on her father's face. He seemed to be enjoying playing detective, but it was a look at the crime scene itself.

Maggie answered for them both. "We're in, Tag. Anything we should know?"

"Just don't let the driver murder anyone on the place if you can. I've had enough trouble out there for a lifetime."

Maggie did laugh this time. "I'll see what I can do."

Chapter Eighteen

Sheriff Wakefield took another turn around the car. There wasn't much more information to be gleaned from it, but the tow company was running late and he was getting bored. There was always the possibility that something might have been missed.

It was just as likely that some new evidence would spring from the ground and introduce itself. The car was still covered with dusting powder, every inch of it was checked, but it was a rental. There were at least seven distinctive fingerprints on the car since it had been washed. It would take hours just to find out which sets of prints they didn't need to bother tracking down.

As far as rentals went, this was a nice car. More mid-life crisis than IRS auditor, it spoke more to bragging than to speed or prestige.

He heard a motor coming and for a moment, he had the hope that the tow truck was finally here. He would be freed from his vigilance, but the engine sounded too small, too light for a truck. When Maggie's car came into view, he suppressed a smile. Officially, she was interfering with police business, but she did have some good insights. And it was always a pleasure to see her even if they had been on the outs recently. Who knew, maybe he'd even have a chance to accept her apology for running up his credit card bill. He had to hand it to her though. Thirty-four crème brulees? It had been a creative method of payback.

Or just maybe he ought to do some apologizing of his own. Neither one of them had been at their best when they'd last talked.

He strained against the glare of the sun on her windshield to see who was with her. If it was Taggart, they would both be leaving and fast. It was bad enough to have Maggie here, but Tag he couldn't justify. It was a pleasant surprise to see her father, but it was definitely a surprise. There was a certain discomfort with having him here, not because of the crime scene as being with Maggie in front of her father seemed...well, different.

"Hello sheriff." Maggie's father strode forward with his hand outstretched like he was running for office. Come to think of it, Wakefield would have gladly voted for him should he ever decide to run for mayor. He shook his hand and then greeted Maggie with a nod. He wasn't sure if her father knew about their spat. In case it was an issue, he decided to play it carefully.

Maggie solved that question by greeting him with a hug. Not an apology, but a truce. Fair enough. He could live with that.

"They haven't showed yet?" She clarified with a tilt of her head to the car. Wakefield could see her reflection in the paint, but more importantly, he could see her father's expression too. He looked pleased with himself. It felt as though Wakefield had passed a test of some sort.

Wakefield shook his head. "No, they gave me an ETA of 20 minutes a half hour ago." Granted, there was a pretty good distance to travel and ten minutes wasn't exactly grounds for a lawsuit. He had been out here too long already, and it rubbed at him that someone should think so little of his time. The impatience must have shown in his voice, because she gave him a quick look and reached out to touch his arm in a reassuring manner. That seemed to help, at least some. He could feel a great deal of his resentment ease under her grasp.

Maggie gave him a final squeeze and let go of his arm. She turned to the car and stared at it much longer than the car warranted. In fact, she tilted her head and stood for a moment, seemingly studying it very closely in that bird dog way she had of scrutinizing things. She even paced the length of the car, every panel coming under her careful examination. He followed her with interest as she ran her hands over the surface, ignoring the dirt and soot that came off on her fingers. Whatever she was looking for, she didn't find it. Maggie hurried around to the other side of the car and repeated the same dance. Her hands were nearly black by the time she finished.

Wakefield turned to her father, but Mr. Wilkerson looked as confused as the sheriff felt. The two men shared a bewildered shrug and turned their attention back to Maggie.

"There are no scratches on this car!" She pointed an accusatory finger at the vehicle.

"Rentals usually don't..." Wakefield ventured then stopped when he realized how pale she'd gone. "Are you alright, Maggie?"

"I..." she looked for a moment as though she were lost. Her glance turned to her dirty hands as though only just noticing them. She turned them around and held them away from her clothes. "I think I need the restroom." She lifted her hands to show him the grime and grinned sheepishly. It was like sunshine breaking through storm clouds. Wakefield let a smile play across his lips.

"The office is locked," Wakefield fished in his pockets, "but I have a key. I'll let you in if I can trust you to behave."

"Scout's honor." She made a haphazard boy scout salute and followed him to the door. He unlocked it and ushered her in front of him. From there, they continued to the office. That was not locked, but he held the door for her anyway before following. Here he nearly collided with her, she stopped so quickly. He wasn't surprised at her reaction; he had done the same when he entered the first time. The place was startling to say the least.

"Yeah," he gestured to the room inside. "Whoever was here, they were looking for something." It was probably the most obvious thing he could have said short of "water is wet." But the remarkable interior needed commenting on. He stopped to look again at the walls. What was left of them. There were pieces of drywall missing. Great sections where the studs were clearly visible, as though someone randomly and methodically carved rough squares from the wall. Some looked as though they were excised by a knife, others had been bashed and torn from their nails. The debris lined the floor with dust and the torn pieces. Whoever had done this was unconcerned about the fallout.

"I tried asking Tag what could have possibly been in the walls that anyone could want, but he hasn't been cooperative."

Maggie didn't answer. She just kept staring, even wavering now slightly on her feet as if in shock.

Frowning now, he continued, "I just don't see it. If there was anything of value, why bury it behind a wall so you can't get to it again? At least not without going to an extreme like this."

He was prodding her and probably shouldn't, but he needed her to speak up and tell him what was wrong. He was missing something here, and he didn't like not knowing what it was.

Finally, he just asked her outright. "Maggie? Are you alright? You look white as a sheet."

She stood still, her eyes wide, her hands at her sides, forgotten. There was a look of panic in her gaze and maybe a hint of something more. Something...sad and disappointed.

"Maggie, what is it? What's wrong? I can get your father if you're feeling ill..."

"No..." Her voice seemed to come from somewhere very far away. When she glanced at him, her smile was forced. "I better get cleaned up so I can get going as soon as the car is gone. After all, that's what we're here for, right?"

He stared at her, knowing she was hiding something. Helpless to figure out what it was short of arresting her.

"Right. The bathroom is right through there." He pointed and watched her go before turning to survey the mess all over again.

What in the world did she see that he hadn't?

Dang but she was an infuriating woman.

Chapter Nineteen

How Wakefield didn't suspect she was up to something, she never knew. Maggie somehow held it together until the tow truck came and took away Gertler's car. She even managed to hold her peace while she drove her father home, though he kept looking at her strangely as if he knew something was up. He likely did, he was sharp, but he kept his calmness.

The problem was, she had two revelations in a matter of minutes which had made no sense at all when considered together.

The first was positive proof that Garrett had been lying to her about the argument with Gertler. There had been no mark on the car. Nothing. What other deceptions had Garrett been saying? Was he lying to Mindy too? That begged the question of whether or not to tell her.

Okay, fine. She would deal with that later. Right now, there were more pressing issues.

It was the second revelation which really bothered her. The one which was taking her now to the only house on the street which had a pitted and destroyed yard full of holes. A house stripped down to the studs.

She was out of the car almost before she had stopped moving. Frantic, she just about pelted to the front door, ringing the bell and calling Doxie's name until the woman appeared.

Doxie seemed smaller, her faithful smile faint. It was almost as if she had always known sooner or later she would be confronted by someone about what she had done.

"Were you hunting for Everett's million dollars out at Space Y?" Maggie asked as soon as Doxie had ushered her inside.

"Oh, my dear..." Doxie sighed, and the lines on her face relaxed, the first hint of her true more upbeat, positive self emerging for the first time in days. "I have been looking *everywhere*." Maggie could hear the exhaustion in her voice.

"What about at the old hunting club? Where Tag is building Space Y? You tore up the old lodge, didn't you?" *Please let me be wrong about this.*

Doxie pursed her lips as she considered her answer. "I might have been..."

"On the night Gertler was killed?" Maggie pressed, her hands knotting the strap of her purse just because she had to hold something right now.

"Maybe." The admission came quietly. Hesitant.

Maggie sucked in a breath. Had the answer truly been here all along, right before her very nose? "Tell me what happened. *Please.*"

Doxie couldn't seem to sit still. She got up and paced around the room, stepping carefully over strewn possessions and bits of drywall. "I didn't mean to make such a mess." She looked around at the debris at her feet and sighed. "Anywhere. Not here. Not there. I just...it got out of control, this need to find the money." Doxie looked more embarrassed than guilty.

"Why the hunting club?" Maggie asked, reaching out to catch the other woman's hand, and drawing her down to sit next to her on the couch. Doxie obeyed mechanically, like a tired child.

"Everett used to spend time out there, back before Tag was old enough to take possession of it. He was the keeper of it, until Tag came of age. I suppose there's a more legal term for that. But he also liked it out there. There was one neighbor, and a couple others, who would just sit out there by the lake for hours. Oh, they'd call it hunting, but they mostly just talked big and stayed out from underfoot of their wives once they retired. I thought..."

"You thought he might have left the money out there, where he'd had such good times," Maggie said when Doxie couldn't seem to finish, and the older woman nodded.

"I went out to look...it took more than one trip to examine the place properly. I'm afraid Tag got rather upset over the mess..."

"He thought someone was vandalizing the place," Maggie said, thinking about the accusations brought against Sam and his reaction to them. No wonder the grouchy neighbor was so mad.

"Anyway, someone came out as I was leaving. Toward evening. I saw the car and thought for sure I was going to be caught. I hid back in the building until I saw the little bald man get out of his car. I was glad it wasn't Tag, as I knew he'd only get upset, though I thought the money might help him. The last thing I expected was for the man to come into the building."

"He saw you?"

"I might have startled him." Doxie winced at this. "I was in the shadows. He must have thought I was a ghost or something the way he turned tail and ran outside like that. I started to follow to explain but then I heard the shotgun blast—"

"Shotgun blast?" This was new.

Doxie nodded miserably. "To think that little man died because I startled him like that. I'm a killer and if I don't find that money I'll never be able to pay for my defense. I don't want to go to JAIL!" The last was said on a woeful shriek. Doxie's hand began to shake.

Maggie grabbed Doxie's arm just as she started to cry. "Jail? Are you kidding? You didn't have anything to do with anything. Gertler didn't die because of you. For one thing, he was shot with an arrow – not by a gun. Whatever you heard had nothing to do with Gertler's death."

"An arrow?" Doxie sniffled and dabbed at her eyes with a tissue. "Are you sure?" A ray of something like hope took hold in her eyes.

"Positive!" Maggie thought a moment, wondering about shell casings or other evidence which might help to save Tag and Doxie both from being wrongfully accused of Gertler's death. "What about your metal detector – did you use that too when you were out there?"

Doxie shook her head. "I didn't find much. Just odds and ends. People drop things, throw them out...it's not really worthwhile."

"Did you keep any of them?"

"It's just junk. Hang on." Doxie got unsteadily to her feet and tottered up the stairs. She came back down a few minutes later with a shoebox tucked under her arm which she handed to Maggie. "I don't see how it can possibly help..."

Maggie studied the contents of the box. Bullet casings made up about half the items there, which made sense given the place had been a hunting club. Added to this was a handful of loose change, an elaborate earring, several nails and bottle caps, and even a couple of toy cars.

Wait.

Maggie fished the earring out of the box. Several shells and stones caught the light. She'd seen this before.

And the owner had nothing to do with Garrett or anyone else.

"Can I keep this?" she asked when she could find her voice.

Doxie waved the object away. "Get rid of it. Not much use to me." She barely glanced at the thing.

Maggie pocketed the earring and told Doxie goodbye. At the doorway though, she paused, because someone needed to say it.

"Get help, Doxie. Please. You can't keep..." She gestured at the broken wall nearest her. "It's not worth it. Not for any amount of money." The woman looked on the edge of a complete break from reality and was frightening Maggie. She didn't have time just then, so she had to trust that Doxie would get help.

Doxie looked at her with watery eyes. "Trying to fix me too?" she asked as she tried to smile. It was slow and thin, but it was there.

"Too?"

"It's what you do. Fixing people. With these mysteries you solve."

She hadn't really thought about it that way. It made her sound almost noble. Maggie decided she wasn't comfortable with that. "I think I just want to see wrongs righted. You know? No one should have to live with an unfair accusation hanging over them." *I've been there too many times.*

"Tag really didn't do it?" The older woman looked more curious than anything.

"No. He didn't."

Maggie knew who did though, and it was someone she should have suspected a long time ago.

In the meantime, she needed to go, and quickly.

Chapter Twenty

The answer had been there all along. Now, as Maggie hurried to the one place she knew she could find her quarry, she tried to think what to say. How do you confront someone with murder? Worse, how do you confront the person who was your first best friend with murder?

Janet was at the park, exactly where she'd spent every afternoon since coming back to town. Maggie stood on the edge of the sidewalk for a long time just looking at her, trying to figure it all out. In her hand was the earring. By itself, it wasn't great evidence. An earring could be lost anywhere and picked up by someone else. Easy to plant if one were to try and cast blame on someone else.

But Janet had slipped up too many times in other ways. In fact, it was all right there in her social media, the name she used online was Holly Chilton, with the jewelry being sold to support the Chilton Foundation.

The very foundation she was touting now to the bored moms watching their children play on the equipment.

If Maggie had only looked at what Janet had been doing that day in the coffee shop, instead of ignoring all the social media stuff her old friend had been trying to push on her, she would have known instantly her friend was the killer.

I just wasn't paying attention. Not where I should have been.

Not that there hadn't been other clues. Janet had claimed to not know Gertler, but of course, she would have. She'd been friends with Sadie. Her little brother had been at every game. Denying it...well it all seemed obvious now.

Maggie swallowed hard. She was only delaying the inevitable. She should call the sheriff, but still she hesitated. What if she was wrong?

No, she wanted to be wrong.

Maggie started across the grass, heading directly for the park bench where Janet held court. Holding up necklaces and earrings, no doubt talking about the good work the women in Africa were doing to get ahead. A noble cause which was only a front for a lavish lifestyle and a need to leave her husband for better things.

The women flocking around Janet were Maggie's customers. Some were becoming friends. How much would they lose in Janet's scheme if she said nothing? She had no time to lose.

"Holly! Holly Chilton!"

She shouted the name, not really knowing what to expect. Janet's head came up instantly, and that told her she'd been heard. Noticed. Janet seemed confused and then, as Maggie held up the earring in one hand, terrified.

More terrified than she'd ever seen another human being.

Janet bolted from the bench, shoving at the woman who surrounded her. One fell, two others got tangled in a stroller. Janet in the meantime, bolted for the parking lot on the opposite end of the park. Leaving behind her children who'd been playing up until this moment, on some kind of low climbing thing nearby.

What was worse, hearing the children's piteous cries as their mother abandoned them, or the knowledge that she'd once called this...this *murderer* a friend? Maggie took off after her, feet pounding the ground, hair flying in the wind.

"Janet, STOP!"

But Janet wasn't listening. She dodged, and she wove. She knocked over a garbage can in her wake, but Maggie was far enough back that she just went around. The problem was, Janet was quite simply in better shape than she was. Apparently, the world of the influencer allowed for regular visits to the gym.

For Maggie, quick walks from her father's home to the bakery where she was surrounded by sweets all day wasn't always conducive to fitness.

Still, she tried. She put her head down and ran for all she was worth, occasionally shouting Janet's name, but Janet paid no heed. She reached the parking lot and kept going. In a second, she would charge right out into the busy street.

No, it wasn't busy by New York standards, but there were cars coming and Janet no longer seemed to be paying attention to them.

"Janet, don't! Don't!" Maggie was behind her still, closer but too far to grab her. A delivery truck was trundling along and any second now—

Maggie shrieked, skidding to a halt on the curb, shielding her eyes even as she heard the scream of brakes, the shouts, the thud of doors slamming shut.

And Janet's voice. Shouting imprecations at the top of her lungs.

Unbelieving, Maggie cracked an eye open and looked.

Garrett was half lying on Janet, pinning her to the sidewalk. He had to have tackled her at the last minute. But why? And where had he come from?

Maggie jogged over, breathing hard, just in time to help Janet up. Not that Janet wanted her help. She jerked her arm out of Maggie's grasp and tried to make a run for it a second time, but Garrett had her firmly. Nor was he alone in the situation. In that moment, Sheriff Wakefield arrived and took charge.

"Sheriff, she killed…"

"Hush, Maggie, I know. Now let me read the woman her rights."

Maggie backed off, but not before she saw the absolute hate in the other woman's eyes. Whatever she'd done, she had felt justified in doing it, if the set chin and her steely gaze had anything to do with it.

In the meantime, Maggie couldn't go. Not when Janet's children were running from the playground crying for their mother.

One of the other moms came after them, grabbing one child while Maggie grabbed the other. "I had a bad feeling about her when she kept pushing for us to invest quickly. A lot of money, all in cash. But these poor moppets don't need to know any of that. This wasn't their fault," she said.

Maggie nodded, unable to speak past the lump in her throat. With the little girl filling her arms and wailing all the while, it was hard to feel good about any of this. So many lives had been ruined by one awful, selfish action. She could only watch with this stranger, waiting until the town's only woman cop showed up with a social worker in tow to take charge of these children who had likewise lost everything in a single day.

The case was over. It was only a matter of tying up loose ends.

Oh, and finally having the Grand Opening which she'd put off far too long. Wasn't that this weekend? She was going to need some help.

"Do you need him?" she asked a cop, pointing a finger at Garrett who was still hovering in the thick of things.

"Not right now. We have his statement and know where to find him if we do need him."

Well, that was more than she knew about him right now.

Maggie grabbed Garrett by the arm, dragging him away from the cops and chaos. "You, my friend, have some serious explaining to do," she informed him as she towed him past Wakefield who was giving her that look he gave her when she meddled in his crime scenes. "But first you have six dozen cupcakes to frost."

He didn't even fight her. That might have had something to do with the fact that Mindy had joined the growing crowd with Bobby at her side. He seemed to be trying real hard to not look like he had any part in this, when it was clear he was up to his neck in the whole thing.

Biscotti served up with a side of betrayal.

Right. Business as usual at Sweet Escapes.

Epilogue

Wakefield tugged at his tie. It didn't feel right to have a knot at your throat and leave the ends dangle for someone to grab, but it was a special occasion. After all the planning and false starts, Maggie's bakery was finally having its Grand Opening. He was proud of her, proud to be with her, but her night was finally going to begin in just a few minutes. At the moment, it was time to wrap a few things up.

"Thank you for coming early." He addressed the small group, Mindy looked stunning in her dress, though it was rather short. Maggie was all dressed up too, likely the last time she would wear something so formal to work at her bakery. Even Bobby was wearing a miniature suit, though it was plain to see he was outgrowing it.

The bow tie on the dog's collar was a bit much.

"There are some things that need to be cleared up." He turned his gaze to Garrett and crossed his arms over his chest. Garrett had offered to stay for the Grand Opening and cook. So, he was the only one dressed casually. Wakefield imagined that Garrett was the only one comfortable too. He tugged at the tie again. "Let's start with who you really are."

Garrett looked around the room at the expectant faces and sighed. "I'm an undercover agent for the IRS. The equivalent of internal affairs." He waited while his audience settled again. "I came to observe Gertler's operations. The head office had suspected him of graft and blackmail, and I was sent to figure out just what was going on."

"Let me guess," Maggie broke in. "Complaints from a certain prisoner we visited who seemed to think he'd been framed."

"Hurley? That's part of it. That list you were working from was part of a much longer document. He wasn't the only one to go to jail after paying off Gertler to look the other way." Garrett grimaced. "There are thirteen individuals doing time right now or who wound up paying hefty fines to the government despite trying to get Gertler to look the other way."

Mindy gasped. "Thirteen? It's no wonder you were called in to investigate."

"But why Tag's case?" Maggie asked.

"We'd already received a tip that there were some pretty heavy duty investors looking at Space Y. We needed to make sure things were being handled correctly. At the same time, it seemed like the perfect opportunity to catch Gertler red handed."

"You used my dad as bait?" Bobby broke in.

"Hush, Bobby..."

Garrett shifted awkwardly. "In a sense. We never thought he would be in any danger or we never would have done it. But in essence, yes we did."

The group looked at each other. None of them seemed particularly happy with this revelation. It was Maggie's father who broke the awkward silence. "So...Do all agents learn to bake like that?" Mr. Wilkerson asked.

"Only the good ones." Garrett grinned. "The truth is, I worked my way through college at a bakery. I got kind of good at it. When I saw you were hiring, I thought it was the perfect cover."

Maggie shook her head and smiled. "You ever want a real job, look me up."

"So..." Mindy spoke with great hesitation and in a small voice. "Was dating me just another...fact-finding mission?"

Garrett had the decency to look embarrassed. "At first, getting to know you was an expedient, but after Gertler died, I...J didn't *need* to, Taggart wasn't under investigation, but I...I wanted to. I just liked being around you. I guess it...I mean..."

Wakefield watched open-mouthed as an undercover specialist became shy and tongue-tied. As for Mindy, she was blushing and seemed to be pulling her head down between her shoulders. He knew that feeling well. He stole a glimpse at Maggie who was looking at him. Yeah, they probably looked just as cute together. Or at least he hoped they did.

In the meantime, it was time to stage a rescue. If they didn't get on with things, the bakery would be crowded with people celebrating the official Grand Opening and there would still be questions left unanswered.

"Garrett, get on with it!" Wakefield called. The baker looked relieved to be rescued from his current state.

"Sorry. Anyway...that was why I was here."

"You lied about the car," Maggie pointed out, "There were no scratches on it. Just a flat tire."

"I'd been following Gertler and he'd seen me several times. This is a small town. To have two strangers in the same place over and over through the town arouses suspicion. Gertler spotted me, demanded to know why I was following him, even threatened to call..." he gestured to Wakefield. "I had to think of some excuse to tell him or my cover would have been blown."

"What did you tell him?" Mr. Wilkerson broke into the silence.

Garrett cleared his throat. "That...well, that he reminded me of someone I used to know, and I was trying to figure out how to ask him for the $200 he owed me. Then when he said he didn't owe me any money, I called him a thief and told him he might as well keep it because I scratched his car in the parking lot anyway. Let's just say things escalated from there." He waited until the chuckling died down and then touched his eye gingerly. "So, as you see, the story was not a complete lie."

He had to wait for the laughter to die down before he could continue.

"After Gertler died, well...I stayed on to see if I could learn anything about him that might make a difference for the people he threatened and harassed. And I couldn't leave without seeing the Grand Opening. I worked too hard for this..."

"*You* worked?" Maggie said in mock outrage. Garrett laughed. Maggie gave him a hug and whispered, "Forget the excitement and travel and livable wage and come work for me."

Garrett laughed. "You have no idea what a temptation that is." He was looking at Mindy when he said it. She blushed again.

"Something I don't understand." Maggie held up a hand, "If a special investigator for the IRS was watching him...how did he get himself killed? How did that get by you?"

Garrett shrugged and pointed to his eye. "After confronting Gertler directly the way I did, I had to back away or my cover would be blown. I had to walk away for a while. That night, I watched Gertler get his dinner and go to his hotel room, I figured he was done for the night, so I left." He looked contrite. "It never occurred to me that he would go to Space Y that late in the day."

"And that was when Gertler surprised Doxie." Maggie took up the tale. "She had moved her search inside by then. When she surprised him, he tried to leave and that's when the shot rang out. The bullet missed him, but flattened the tire."

"I thought it was an arrow," Mindy interrupted. "Was that the killer?"

"No." Wakefield answered, "That was just Sean. In the dusk, he saw a man leaving, thought it was Taggart. Sean was trying to scare him, make him think it wasn't worthwhile to hold onto the property. He thought taking a potshot at Tag would scare him a little. Make him more eager to sell. I talked to him after interviewing Doxie. Until then, I couldn't get a confession out of him. But knowing he'd been seen...well he sang like a canary. Didn't want to be blamed for murder. Said the only thing he killed was the tire on the car that was parked there. He said he only knew he'd blown things when he recognized Doxie coming out after the other guy. Sean ran so he wouldn't be caught, figuring he was in a world of trouble."

"Which explained the flat tire on Gertler's car," Maggie guessed.

"Forensics took a closer look at the tire after the car was moved. Sure enough there was a bullet hole they hadn't seen initially because it was between the tread."

"So, after Sean fired the shot, what happened to Gertler?" Mindy asked, happier now that Garrett was holding her hand.

Wakefield started warming to his topic, "Doxie left in a hurry, we think Gertler dove into some bushes for cover. We found a patch of flattened grass which would be consistent with that."

"So..." Maggie was thinking out loud, "How did Janet come into this?"

"Well..." Wakefield thought for a moment. "I suppose I can tell you." He glanced over at Mr. Wilkerson who nodded. Legal bases covered, he continued, "She confessed to everything in a plea for leniency. It'll be common knowledge soon enough. She saw him driving out of town that night, and followed Gertler to see where he was going. When he parked at Space Y, she saw it as an opportunity to talk to him on neutral ground. See, she'd gone to his room to talk to him there, but they didn't do much talking."

"That's unexpected," Mr. Wilkerson put in. "Tell me he wasn't blackmailing her into..." He gave a look in the direction of Bobby who was playing with the dog and no longer paying any attention.

Wakefield leaned on the counter. "Not at all. She had been seeing him for some time, ever since she was audited. It seems he got her out of trouble with the IRS. She thought that meant he loved her. She really did have feelings for the little creep. Only it looks like the affection was more one-sided than she realized. That night, in his hotel room, she took a shower..."

"That explains why a bald man would have used shampoo!" Maggie interrupted.

"Right, it was hers. Anyway, she asked him for financial help to leave her husband, only he laughed and told her *she* was going to pay *him,* or he would be sure she lost custody of the kids in her divorce."

"I'll bet that was unexpected after all the help he'd been giving her. Any idea why he'd turned on her?" Maggie asked.

Wakefield shrugged. "Who's to say. Maybe he freaked a little when he found out she was leaving her husband. It sounded like she was thinking matrimony with Gertler once the dust from the divorce settled. Might be he was just tired of her. We can't exactly ask and she only sees things the way she wants to."

"But it had to shock her, finding out that he was not only going back on her, but asking her for money as well," Maggie mused.

Wakefield agreed. "She got desperate then and started milking wealthy mothers in the area. She started by stealing purses at the park, out of diaper bags. At some point she started thinking, what was in their wallets was small potatoes compared to what was in their bank accounts. She was setting them up for a more sizable conquest, a massive donation to that fake charity of hers."

"Fake?" Maggie echoed.

"It's nothing but a web page. She'd been running that scam for years."

"That's why her purse didn't go with her outfit." Mindy turned to Maggie, her eyes wide. "It was probably stolen."

"Anyway," Wakefield took charge again, "She found the crossbow and suddenly had an idea how to end Gertler's tyranny. When he saw her there, he likely thought it meant he was safe and went to greet her, but by then, it was too dark to see the crossbow, so she shot him at point blank range."

"So, she didn't need to be an expert shot, she was already close." Garrett sounded impressed.

"Right." Wakefield paused while the others thought on this. He was about to ask if anyone was still confused when the door burst open.

"GUYS! You won't believe this! We're going to have a launch pad! We're going to put small satellites into space!"

"Tell us something we don't already know," Mindy said, laughing. "You told us about your oh-so-famous connections a few days ago."

Tag grabbed her and whirled her around, much to the astonishment of almost everyone there. Garrett just looked peeved.

"No, this is different. A sure thing. I just *signed* the *papers*, it's *official*! I have to tell my investors, but I wanted all of you to be the first to know! I did it. I really did it!" Taggart turned to Mindy and kissed her before finally letting her go. He ruffled Bobby's hair, kissed Maggie's cheek, and shook her father's hand. He even patted Benny on the head too.

He turned and held his hand out for the sheriff to shake. Stunned, Wakefield did just that.

"Gotta go!" Taggart waved as he fled through the door. The rest of them looked at each other as if to find verification that it really happened. As if on cue, they all burst into bemused laughter.

"All right!" Maggie called, "Guests will be here any moment now. Let's be ready!"

The group broke up. Garrett retreated to the kitchen. Mindy, after a word with Bobby, followed him. Bobby simply headed over to the table where the goodies were. Wakefield saw him stuffing sweets into his pockets and decided the crime was outside of his jurisdiction.

He had more important things to deal with.

Wakefield pulled the star of the evening aside, "Maggie, I'm sorry if I was rough on you. It's just that...I worry about you. I cannot tell you how much you mean to me. I..." he leaned over and gave her a kiss. It was quick in case she objected. To his delight, she didn't.

"How did you know to come when you did?" Maggie was blushing as she asked him this.

Wakefield shrugged off the question. "Quite simple, really, I saw Janet's Insta when I went to look at your page. I saw the name, matched it to Gertler's laptop, and there it was." He grinned at her look of consternation. "See? I really am good at my job."

"Yes, you are." Maggie said slyly. "With a little help."

"Hey!"

Maggie laughed and pulled the door open to the waiting crowd outside.

"Welcome to our Grand Opening!"

If she crowed a little, she'd earned it. He only hoped that whatever her next adventure turned out to be, he would be right there with her.

Life was certainly interesting with Maggie Wilkerson around.

THE END

If you enjoyed Bows & Bitter Betrayals, you will love Clues & Cruel Catastrophes.

(Click here to get Clues & Cruel Catastrophes)

Holly's father passed away, so she decides to move back to her hometown to re-open the family diner. Little did she know, someone would be framing her for murder. Molly and her best friend are unraveling the clues to prove her innocence and uncover the secrets her father left behind...Read Chapter One on the next page!

Sneak Peek

Finding a dead woman that had drifted to shore right outside the diner, isn't how she anticipated her re-opening day.

When Holly Middleton's father passed away, the family's business died alongside him. The diner was very well loved by the community. Holly didn't realize how the closing of the diner would impact her, so she packed up her stuff in New York and was looking forward to her new start.

Once she was back in her hometown, she couldn't wait to re-open the diner again.

She soon realized someone was framing her for the murder of Annalisa Rice, owner of the rival diner in town. Sheriff Carlton, who didn't seem to like Holly much, jumped at the chance to arrest her.

Holly and Scarlet, her loose-lipped best friend, are unraveling the clues in order to prove her innocence. Small towns talk, and right now, the talk in town is not looking good for Holly's return.

Once the murder is solved, she can get back to building the diner of her dreams, but first she must uncover the secrets her father left behind.

It's a rat race against time to find out who the real killer is before Holly ends up in the grave next to Annalisa.

(Click here to get Clues & Cruel Catastrophes)

"Look who's back in town." The familiar light-breezy tone murmured behind Holly made her freeze in her stride that Sunday afternoon. It didn't take much for her to figure out who was behind her. Holly spent the past few years speaking to the woman nearly every day over the phone.

The cool afternoon sea-breeze ruffled Holly's hair as a small smile spread out on her lips. Holly heard the whoosh of ocean waves as it crashed into the shores a few feet away from them, and the sound smoothed over her. It released a euphoric feeling of serenity that she always enjoyed.

Perks of living in a beach town. Holly especially loved the view of the beach from her room upstairs, above the diner. She never grew tired of it.

"Scarlet," Holly greeted as she turned around and spread her arms wide for her best friend's hug.

"It's good to have you back," Scarlet murmured as they hugged tightly, both cradling each other close.

"It's good to be back," she moved away from her friend a little. She brushed off some strands of hair from her face and tucked them behind her ear. "I never thought I'd say this, but I missed Cleverly Shores. I missed you even more."

"Aww..." Both women chuckled as they hugged again, and Holly took the time to admire her friend once she stepped back.

"What has it been, five years? Not much has changed since you've been gone, trust me. Cleverly Shores is just as you remember it."

"All of it?" Holly lead Scarlet inside the diner she spent her entire morning cleaning. The place was a dusty mess. Every corner and floorboard needed cleaning. The windows were blackened by years of dirt. Holly had contemplated hiring a cleaning company at first, but then she decided to just get it done herself.

She had started out in the kitchen, then worked her way through the rest of the dining area, till she got to the front porch.

"Well maybe not all of it. There's been a few developments," Scarlet answered with a cheery laugh. "At least we've got a bigger park now. Oh right, and there's a bonfire this Wednesday night. You should come to that and meet up with some of the people in the community. It'll give you an opportunity to catch up with some people you haven't seen in years and let them know you are back to stay. I know it will be a good time."

Inside the diner now, Scarlet looked around. "You're working magic here already. This place has been out of business for a long time. It's hard to even remember what the recipes taste like."

"Well, not for long," Holly told her as she lifted a box of cleaning supplies from the ground and placed them on the table. "I'm back now! And I'm starting up Frijole's again. I should have it up and running in just a couple days. Thankfully, there's not much to fix up besides the broken pipes in the kitchen. The bonfire night sounds like the perfect chance to let the town know I'm back in business, don't you think? I'll definitely be there."

Scarlet nodded, "Well, if you need any help, I'm always a ring away. Frijole's has always been my favorite diner. Your dad's enchiladas can't be compared to any others, not even Double Flavors. Ever since your dad shut down the diner, Annalisa Rice's restaurant has become a franchise without competition."

The mention of Frijole's rich competition reminded Holly a little of the last time she was here in Cleverly Shores. She recalled the day like it just happened, even though it was five years ago. Annalisa wasted no time at all coming over and relished in the fact that the diner had to temporarily close due to some licensing issues.

"She still walks around town gloating to everyone about how successful her business is. Everyone knows her husband funded the entire thing from scratch, but who cares? She's the boss. Always has been."

Scarlet took off the shawl wrapped around her neck and eased herself down on one chair. Holly realized her friend was just as she remembered. Brown hair cropped to her shoulders just like Holly's, and a vibrant shade of brown eyes. Scarlet's ever standing grin spread out wider as she stared at Holly with excitement.

"Want to know something even better," Scarlet continued with her gossip. Holly noticed that her friend's penchant for gossip still remained the same. It lured a smile onto Holly's lips as she pulled out a chair for herself. "Annalisa got divorced. She cheated on Mr. Rice...Big scandal and he filed for a divorce. It was messy, trust me. The entire town knew about it."

"Wow, a lot really has happened," Holly whispered as she took all of Scarlet's info in all at once.

Holly's mind was still processing when she heard the nearby rev of a car's engine. She stood up, walked to the window, and stared outside to see a white Mercedes pull up in front of her property.

"Expecting someone?" Scarlet came over to stand by Holly's side and gasped once the car door opened and the driver stepped out. "Speak of the devil. Why is Annalisa visiting you?"

"To gloat?" Holly suggested and Scarlet scoffed in return. "Who knows? It's not like Annalisa's that unpredictable."

Holly's sentence was barely complete when the front door swung open. Her presence instantly filled the air with the thick citrusy scent of her perfume. The woman was just as Holly remembered her. Tall, with a model like slenderness, and platinum blonde hair she liked to wear cropped short to her neck. Her eyes are the same mariner blue.

They have a chilled feel each time she stared at someone, and Holly was never able to be at ease around her, even in the past.

Holly muffled a sigh as she remembered sneaking into the Rice's beach mansion during the summers to spend time with their son Timothy. The fond memories of their short-lived romance warmed her heart for a few seconds. Immediately, she shrugged off the nostalgic feeling before it took over. Holly rarely ever thought of Timothy. Not after how she ended their romance and left Cleverly Shores without saying goodbye.

"Holly," Annalisa greeted with a cheery smile that didn't reach her eyes. "It's so good to see you again, dear. When I heard the rumors that you were back in town, I couldn't believe it."

"It's nice to see you too, Mrs. Rice. You look good as always."

"Thanks dear."

"Hello, Mrs. Rice," Scarlet greeted with a wave, but she barely spared her a glance and responded with a small nod.

Holly and Scarlet fell quiet as her piercing eyes scanned the entire dining area. She held a designer purse in her left hand, and her right hand sat on her hip with poise.

"This place is just as I remember it," she commented before her eyes settled on Holly again. "It's going to take a lot to bring this place back to life, and even with all the repairs you might have to do, it still won't be up to standard." She smiled as she looked right at Holly, "Cleverly Shores now has standardized restaurants thanks to Double Flavors."

"I heard," Holly responded while keeping her smile. "I'm sure you still serve the best enchiladas anyone in Cleverly Shores has ever tasted."

"Of course," she laughed, and the bubbling cheeriness spiked a little irritation in Holly.

Can the woman's pride get worse than this?

"Trust me dear, it really is the best. I wish you all the luck though. You'll need it to get this place going again."

"Thank you, Mrs. Rice."

She tilted one shoulder up in a carefree shrug, hummed once, then turned and walked out of the door. Once she was gone and out of sight, Holly and Scarlett exchanged knowing looks.

"Told you she was here to brag," Holly said to her friend as they both walked to the window to watch Annalisa drive off.

"You know what? We should visit Double Flavors tonight. Their enchiladas are really not that good." Scarlet frowned as she commented, then rolled her eyes. "Their pizza's the worst. Your crust wasn't that dry on your first try, trust me."

"I don't see Annalisa as competition," She told Scarlet before walking away from the window so she could continue her cleaning. "Besides, Cleverly Shores is big enough to have more than one good Mexican diner, don't you think?"

"Absolutely. That's a great way to think about it," Scarlet agreed just before a long howl speared into the air around them and stopped both of them in their tracks. Holly turned to Scarlet, "Did you hear that?"

"Sounds like a ..." Holly didn't complete her sentence before a tiny bark cut in again. This time, she walked out of the diner, and around the building to check for the noise.

There was a German short-haired pointer wandering around the back yard when Holly and Scarlet arrived. The dog froze for a second once she noticed them, then barked again before rushing towards Holly while wagging her tail.

"That's Mrs. Genesis's dog," Scarlet murmured once the dog neared them and Holly dropped to a squat to gently touch her head.

"Mrs. Genesis, our English teacher in the sixth grade...she passed away a few months ago."

"Oh, that is sad," Holly sympathized while the dog kept wagging her tail. She continued to stroke her head a little, and sighed, "She's probably all alone. Did Mrs. Genesis live by herself?"

"Yeah, she did. And I know this dog meant a lot to her."

"Good dog." The dog started to jump a little, salivate, then jumped around some more. "I think I'm going to keep her. Sounds like we both could use the company."

"You think you can handle a dog on your own?"

"I had a puppy once, remember? They are like kids. All you need to give them is a little love and attention."

Holly ruffled the dog's head some more as she barked and lied on the sandy ground before rolling around in it. "See," she pointed out, "A little love and attention."

Scarlet still looked a bit skeptical. "If you say so," she agreed before folding her hands over her chest. "It's probably not a bad idea since you are all by yourself in the apartment."

Holly smirked at her friend and returned her attention to the playful dog. Scarlet was right, the last time she was in Cleverly Shores, she had her father. Now she was alone. Scarlet was the closest person she had to family, and this dog could be a good companion to have around.

"I'll call her Chile. It's got a nice ring to it."

(Click here to get Clues & Cruel Catastrophes)

Printed in Great Britain
by Amazon